FIVE FOR THE
APOCALYPSE

TS ALAN

Published by TS Alan, 4/20/2021

ISBN: 978-1-7351711-2-8 (softcover)

ISBN: 978-1-7351711-3-5 (ePub)

Edited by Kevin Fern

Cover/inner sketch by John Becaro

Flag artwork by Anton Shevialiukhin & TS Alan

Design by TS Alan

In Memoriam
Kym Carr, Bob Lipman, Don Rinaldo, Susan Spoth

And for all my classmates of Williamsville South High

Special thanks to Paul A. Wiese

CONTENTS

Part I   1

Part II   31

Part III   73

Part IV   113

Part V   127

Part VI   147

Part VII   167

About the Author   187

PART I

CIVIL WAR

THERE WERE BLOODIED, DISMEMBERED CORPSES ALL ACROSS THE WAR-ravaged field. Some bodies were bullet-ridden, others savagely torn apart by artillery, or both. Then there were those who had not yet perished from their horrific injuries. Their haunting and agonizing pleas for help hung heavy in the late morning air. It hadn't mattered what gender you identified as, or what side you were fighting on, the bullets and bombs had been indiscriminate in their maiming, their killing, and their destruction.

A young dismayed corporal, hot with anger and anguish upon his face, stood amongst the dead, shouting obscenities at the retreating enemy. He had not noticed he had been wounded, though his injury was merely a bullet graze to his left triceps, nor that he had soiled himself. He was all consumed with cursing the enemy, for they had mortally wounded and grievously injured so many of his friends and comrades. There had been one soldier in particular that had died in the initial advance. One death that cut him to the quick. It had been Private Carol King. She had been a classmate of his, and he knew her well. Carol had taken a round to her head and was killed instantaneously. It was a bullet that should have struck him but he had slipped and took a tumble. Carol had been behind him. She stopped to help him up. When she turned forward again to continue their advance on the enemy's defensive line, she had been shot; a direct hit to her face. The sight of her bloody, mutilated face made corporal violently sick to his stomach. As he began to puke, his commanding officer began yelling at him to "get his shit together and move your ass, soldier." He had no choice but to do as ordered. By the end of the day the enemy would be routed.

As he stood in the open lobbing obscenities at the enemy that had withdrawn, he hadn't considered possibility of enemy snipers. Another young soldier, a private, came running to him. The private tried to pull the agitated corporal from the front line, but he was met with resistance. The private yelled and vigorously shook his friend to snap him out of his fixation. Finally, understanding the situation and the harm he was placing himself and the private in, they both retreated back to their defensive line. It had been a harrowing battle the two would unfortunately never forget, and one that would define the youths for the rest of their lives; especially the corporal.

———————

When childhood friends Logan Ross and Benny Lee left Delaware Academy Middle/High School after their junior years to join the Middle Colonial Territorial National Guard Reserve, neither could have fathomed they would end up 2,500 miles west of their hometown of Delhi, NY. After all, their brigade was only supposed to be aiding the Army of the Territorial Republic of America in a sustainment capacity—providing services for everyday logistics like fuel, common ammo, medical supplies, repair parts of wheeled vehicles, and so forth —not guarding the southern border of the District of Pennsylvania with the regular soldiers. However, soon after their enlistment, their brigade was integrated into the regular army that was fighting the United Territories of America (UTA) in a civil war.

The catalyst for the civil war had been the worst single pandemic in UTA history. Within six months RSV-47.b infected at least twenty-eight and a half million Americans and killed another 700,000. Every country in the world closed its borders to America.

World leaders had long linked germs and immigrants to stoke fear in moments of crisis. It was no different with Sovereign Arnold Trumbull. His repeated, often inflammatory and extreme political rhetoric of unfounded fears of connections between germs and immigrants charged the xenophobic masses. Trumbull ordered immigration halted and all undocumented foreign nationals living in the country rounded up and placed into quarantine camps. Hate crimes rose to unprecedented levels, the likes of which had never been seen in American history.

Sovereign Trumbull and his administration were ill-prepared for a response to the pandemic. Once there had been a robust UTA pandemic infrastructure, which included epidemic monitoring and a command group inside the Sovereign's Palace Domestic Security Council (DSC) Directorate for Global Health Security and Biodefense, and another in the Homeland Security Sector (HSS)—both of which followed the scientific and public health leads of the National Institutes of Health (NIH) and the Communicable Disease Center (CDC).

However, out of petty retribution for the previous sovereign's failure to re-take the Alaska Territory after it was annexed by Canada in 2029—ultimately leading to the previous sovereign's ousting from office—the government had intentionally rendered itself incapable of a proper response.

Beginning the morning after his oath of sovereignty, a stunning science-related tragedy unfolded. The Trumbull administration systematically began to take apart the previous administration's science infrastructure and rejected the role of science to inform policy. He first fired the government's entire pandemic response chain of command, including the Sovereign's Palace management infrastructure, along with disbanding his Council of Advisors on Science and Technology. Afterward he closed the DSC Directorate for Global Health Security and Biodefense. This was the office that would galvanize resources to coordinate a full-bodied and seamless domestic and global pandemic response. It was led by a senior-level response coordinator who coordinated the high-level domestic and global reporting structure. Next the Sovereign thoroughly dismantled America's remaining response departments by reducing national health spending and cutting the global disease-fighting operational budgets of the CDC, HSS, and Health and Human Services. Plus, the government's $50 million Complex Crises Fund was eliminated.

Furthermore, The United Territories of America federal government had very little infrastructure to ensure the manufacturing of essential goods were met or to aid farmers and ranchers in getting their goods to market during such a crisis. Dairy farmers dumped their milk. Vegetable and fruit farmers harvested their crops and disposed of them by leaving them in massive mounds to rot in their fields. Poultry, cattle and sheep raisers slaughtered and burnt the livestock that they could no longer afford to feed. With a growing famine and the economy in ruins, economists projected the looming financial crisis would be far greater than that of the Great Depression. The dire forecast prompted

Sovereign Trumbull and his neo-fascist regime to push for territories to restart businesses to get people back to work, though the pandemic had barely begun to decline from its peak. At first governors refused, which spawned protests by citizens who defied stay-at-home orders and rallied in front of the territorial capitols of Minnesota, Michigan, and the Districts of Virginia and Georgia in the Southern Colonial Territory, touting that their constitutional rights were being violated.

Arnold Trumbull fired the first shots in the Plague Civil War, a modern-day Jefferson Davis of the Pro-Pandemic Territories of America sending his opening volley from Fort *Status*—Status being the social media platform he so often used to criticize and belittle his opposition—at those governors who dared to question if it wasn't just too early to end the stay-at-home orders in territories still far to the left of the apex. He Statused the following directives: "LIBERATE MINNESOTA!" "LIBERATE MICHIGAN!" "LIBERATE TEXAS AND MISSISSIPPI, and save your great 2nd Amendment. It is under siege!"

In response, most territories loyal to Trumbull did as instructed. But many others still refused, citing that the sovereign was being reckless and irresponsible, and that territorial governors had a duty and obligation to serve their territories and protect their citizens, as they swore to do so upon their oath of office. This then invoked Sovereign Trumbull's rage, and he issued an executive order that all territories were to begin a re-start. Still many declined.

When asked during a press conference on what the UTA government's response was to those governors who refused to obey the executive order, Trumbull told reporters, "When somebody's the Sovereign of the United Territories, the authority is total. And that is the way it's going to be. It's total. And the governors know that… Under the UTA Constitution, the Army National Guard and the Air National Guard of each non-compliant territory can be called forth 'to execute the Laws of the Union, and suppress Insurrections.' It's the Insurrection Act. All I have to do is call them up."

The sovereign's threats were taken seriously. A few more territories fell in line, but the rest formed a coalition, and the coalition met in

Philadelphia, PA, in the New England Colonial Territory. There the fundamental documents of a new government were promulgated, a provisional government was established, and then a representative was sent to Washington, DC to deliver the declaration of secession.

Meanwhile, the new interim Chief of the Territorial Republic of America issued a call for all soldiers from the various territorial national guards to defend the newly formed republic. All United Territories of America property was seized, along with gold and silver bullion and coining dies of any UTA mints within the Territorial Republic. The Republic capital was moved from Philadelphia to Buffalo, New York. Two weeks later, former governor Dennis Scott of the Middle Colonial Territory was inaugurated as chief of the newly formed Territorial Republic of America—simply The Republic.

Now nearly four years into the second American Civil War, the country had been profoundly devastated. The war had become the most lethal conflict in American history; the number of human lives it took did not fully convey the pervasive damage it caused. In every theater, UTA and Republic armies lived off the land, helping themselves to any form of food they could find, animal and vegetable, when needed. These armies were huge, mobile communities that caused an environmental catastrophe of the first magnitude, with effects that would endure long after the guns and bombs were silenced. Both sides destroyed cities, farms and livestock. They fouled waters, spread disease, and bombarded the geography with heavy armaments and left unexploded shells, they left debris and garbage behind. Luckily, both sides agreed not to deploy biological, chemical, or thermonuclear weapons.

The country had been profoundly devastated physically, economically, environmentally, psychologically, and morally. It was no longer a nation, only a state of chaos. Neither side had come out more victorious than the other, and both sides were resolute in seeing their righteous side win.

Indeed, neither Logan Ross nor Benny Lee could have considered they would end up 2,500 miles west of their hometown of Delhi, NY, but they were. Having shown outstanding heroism under unusually adverse conditions and proving their bravery in three different key battles of the war, the two friends and the remainder of their Delaware Brigade—merely two squads—were rewarded by being reassigned from the frontline to a vital rear-guard position.

Having received their fourth field promotions, First Sergeant Ross and Sergeant First Class Lee were assigned to the Ari-Cal-Nev Hoover Dam Joint Task Force as part of their security company to guard and defend the Hoover Dam from the UTA. With the exception of two police consultants, all of the Hoover Dam Police Department's Security Response Force had been reassigned to the smaller Parker and Davis Dams downstream. Whoever held the main dam controlled the reservoir. It was the critical water and power supply for the Arizona, California, and Nevada Territories, all of which were part of The Republic.

There were about 900 troops that made up the battalion sized joint task force, which consisted of a sustainment support company, a quartermaster platoon, an ordinance platoon, a medical platoon, a Corps of Engineers platoon that was assigned to assist dam engineers, and the Hoover Damn Security Force (HDSF). There was even a combat aviation unit assigned to the dam from nearby Nellis Air Force Base (AFB). However, Logan and Benny were no longer the commanders of their Delaware Brigade, which had now become D Platoon of the HDSF. Instead, they found themselves the fourth and fifth highest ranking Senior NCOs of the HDSF. Benny had been assigned the duty position of Platoon Sergeant, who was the primary assistant and advisor to the platoon leader, with the responsibility of training and caring for soldiers. Logan was assigned as the platoon leader, which was highly unusual since that was the job of a lieutenant. However, it had been discovered that Lt Carson was a UTA spy. He was given a quick court-martial, and then immediately executed. In his stead, Logan was given the leadership position, mainly because of his combat experience. That went for Benny as well as those that had served with them in the Delaware Brigade. There had been few in the joint task force under the rank of sergeant that had seen combat. Most of the troops that were serving had come from the tri-territorial militias. Logan and Benny's experience on the battlefield was a valuable asset to the dam task force since they had been infiltrated. A great concern was that the enemy knew all the task force weaknesses, especially about their defensive positions.

Logan and Benny had just finished with their weekly 7:00 a.m. senior staff meeting inside the Spillway House—the joint task force's meeting room—and were on their way back to the Hoover Dam Mercantile Building that contained the operations center, when a high-priority call came in from Nellis AFB. There were intercontinental ballistic missiles inbound, and their trajectory put two on a track for Boulder City and Las Vegas. Nellis also warned that the attack being tracked was part of a massive strike of hundreds of ICBMs that were targeting both UTA and Republic cities, and the multiple bogeys inbound were coming from multiple directions.

Almost every nation in the world still had thermonuclear weapons but no nation had ever deployed them. This was because of a moratorium agreed upon by a majority of the members of the United Nations, when it came to the development of pure fusion weapons. Member nations could keep their nukes as long as they didn't develop pure fusion weapons. The UTA was opposed to the agreement based on humanitarian reasons and voted against it, but it passed anyway.

"This is the most idiotic agreement the United Nations has ever ratified," Ambassador Blocker, the leader of the UT delegation, declared when the act was passed.

The difference between a pure fusion weapon and a thermonuclear warhead was in the fusion reaction. Pure fusion weapons generated small nuclear yields because no critical mass of fissile fuel was needed for detonation, as was needed with a thermonuclear weapon. Yet, they had far greater destructive force. Besides the destructive force, another advantage of a pure fusion weapon was the reduced collateral damage stemming from fallout since a pure fusion weapon did not create the highly radioactive byproducts associated with fission-type weapons. Because of this there was also no electromagnetic pulse produced, as this originates from the gamma rays released by fissioning nuclei. Simply, pure fusion weapons were more destructive but nuclear warheads were more deadly. In protest, Sovereign Trumbull withdrew the UTA's membership, and then shut the United Nations building down and told the intergovernmental organization to find a new home.

The unimaginable scenario of foreign nations launching a thermonuclear weapons strike against America had finally come to fruition —but the Sovereign had been warned. In unity, the member nations of the yearly World Economic Summit, even those aligned with America, issued a statement that the Sovereign's failure and inability to centrally resolve the Respiratory Syncytial Virus (RSV-47) pandemic had exacerbated preexisting global problems and imbalances, and that these could deteriorate to a point where there would be a conflict of "All against America" to stop the global spread. What had once been a common respiratory virus that usually caused mild, cold-like symptoms had mutated into a deadly disease. Just because civil war had broken out in America, didn't mean the virus had been magically vanquished; it was persistent, prevalent, and invasive—and in America it kept mutating.

There was no national mandate from the Sovereign requiring everyone to wear a mask while out in public. Many refused to follow territorial mandates regarding mask use, citing that being forced to comply violated their constitutional rights. When the Republic was formed, Chief Dennis Scott requested everyone within the new country to mask up and do physical distancing to help stop the spread. Still there were those that refused. The UTA developed the first vaccine within a year of the outbreak but the Sovereign refused to give it to The Republic unless they surrendered. The withholding of the vaccine only further solidified The Republic's determination to remain independent. Three months later, The Republic obtained a different serum from Germany. Even with both governments having vaccines, there were anti-vaxxers and conspiracy theorists from both sides spreading misinformation on social media about them containing mind control drugs or monkey brains—monkey brains because a replicant-deficient simian adenovirus vector was used in formulating the vaccine. The UTA government did nothing to act against the propaganda. The Republic's efforts with their public education campaign to counteract the lies was ineffectual. However, the anti-maskers and anti-vaxxers were not the main cause for the second wave of the pandemic, which had a significant, substantial increase in transmissibility and mortality. It was the inability to acquire enough vaccine from Germany. However, the worst was yet to come. The disease mutated yet again. This alteration caused a more severe disease, more hospitalizations, and more deaths. The new strain, designated RSV-47.d, was up to 70% more transmissible than the secondary strain of the disease. In addition, it made people sicker and it changed the way someone's immune system responded to the virus if they were previously infected or vaccinated.

The safest place to survive the blast effects was in the "Gold Room". It was part of the original powerhouse where copper cabinets—brightly polished looking like "gold"—once housed busbars and wires that carried electricity from Hoover Dam's generators to the transformers. But decades ago, the last copper cabinet had been removed as part of a modernization project. The 600-foot-long room that was above the powerhouse was mainly empty. It wasn't an ideal place to hunker down when it came to physically distancing, but it was the safest place to survive the attack.

Hoover Dam wasn't some frail concrete structure that an indirect fission-fusion blast could take out. While the dam was only 45 feet thick at the top and 650 feet thick at its base, the high strength 7200 psi concrete that was used in its construction was reinforced with 45,000,000 pounds of steel. This concrete was not as hard as a missile silo but it was twice as hard as common construction concrete, and there was 4,360,000 cubic yards of it. In total the dam weighed 6.6 million tons. It was a bit more than a bunker. So, if a thermonuclear weapon at full yield airburst above the dam, it would only scorch it, and obliterate anything on it, but leave the dam largely intact. Diversely, if any fission-fusion detonation did occur above, it would radiate and poison the water in the reservoir and the two smaller lower Colorado dams with massive gamma radiation. Also, the electromagnetic emissions would damage the turbines within the power plant, thus rendering the dam unusable.

In the six months Logan and Benny had been assigned to the dam, they had experienced only one grand attack. The attack had come from Hill Air Force Base north of Salt Lake City, Utah and Mountain Home Air Force Base, south of Boise, Idaho. It had been the second time UTA forces had launched simultaneous aerial assaults against Nellis AFB, Boulder City, and the dam. They were part of two different major UTA offensives to push into Nevada and Arizona. Both times the ground and the air offensives had been repelled. The second time the only major damage sustained to the dam area had been to the Mercantile Building, which had been destroyed, and some repairable damage to the short-wave radio installation. Unlike Nellis AFB and Boulder City, the enemy wasn't trying to destroy the dam itself. They were trying to neutralize its defensive capabilities, including the anti-aircraft weapons and long-range canon artillery installations that were placed in camouflaged fortifications on the hills surrounding the dam and bypass bridge. The Mercantile Building was used for billeting. Logan had been asleep in the building when the attack had begun. Everyone asleep that night had made it out of the building but not everyone survived the attack. There had been many wounded; luckily the fatalities were not heavy. Now, they were about to face the biggest assault in their military careers, far more devastating than the Battle of Dubuque, where most of their brigade had met its fate.

An ICBM launched from Korea could strike Los Angeles, California in 38 minutes. In less than a minute after a launch, a space tracking and surveillance satellite would raise the alarm, and the Missile Defense Integration and Operations Center at Schriever Air

Force Base near Colorado Springs, Colorado would be alerted and spring into action. Attack-assessment information received from the satellite and Upgraded Early Warning Radars that detect and track (ICBMs) and Sea Launched Ballistic Missiles (SLBM) at High Pines Air Force Station, Oregon and Beale Air Force Base, California would be quickly analyzed. The warning and attack-assessment data on the missile would also be sent to UTA STRATCOM, the Joint Space Operations Center, and the Missile Warning and Space Control Center.

The command center would send launch orders after determining whether Fort Greely or Vandenberg Air Force Base, California was better-positioned to intercept, using Ground-based interceptor missiles (GBIs). Ground Missile Defense used non-nuclear GBIs with a kinetic warhead. By the time of launch, about eight to ten minutes may have passed since the Korean missile was first detected. Still flying through space, the warhead might be about three-quarters of the way through its journey to America at this point, perhaps 22 minutes, when the ICBM would be intercepted and destroyed.

Except there was a civil war being waged. The Colorado Territory was now occupied by UTA forces. Communications between the two sides were iffy at best. It was a barrage of ICBMs coming from multiple directions, not just a few, and there were only 36 GBIs stashed in silos at the two sites—and Oregon was a UTA territory. Plus, the countermeasure only had a 97% intercept rate. The UTA warning to The Republic of inbound missiles was received but it came late, just as Beale Air Force Base, California, detected them. Then Beale AFB passed on the information onto Vandenberg AFB, California and gave them launch authority.

No one had to explain the close or far reaching effects of a detonated nuclear warhead. Beale AFB notified Nellis AFB. Nellis notified authorities in Las Vegas as well as the Ari-Cal-Nev Hoover Dam Joint Task Force Command, which in turn notified the Boulder City Garrison Command and the two lower dams. That was where the sustainment support company, the quartermaster platoon, the ordinance platoon, and the medical platoon were stationed. By the time everyone was notified, it was estimated that inbound missiles could strike

Boulder City and Nellis within 15-20 minutes. It was 19 minutes travel time from Garrison Command to the dam, once they were ready to depart.

Within an hour of an attack, a plume of radioactive fallout would unfurl 30 miles beyond the city. For all of this, it would be a matter of seconds for the dam to feel its destructive force. Not everyone could fit into the gold room. Some took refuge in operational offices and hallway spaces in a higher part of the dam. Logan wasn't religious but Benny was. He led a prayer session for those who were in need that had made it to the gold room. Tensions and anxieties were high amongst the men and women huddled together. Some became nauseous and vomited from the stress of waiting. Five minutes after the projected attack there was no thunderous shotgun-like boom, sustained roar, or earth-shaking rumble. Another 10 minutes past, still no noise, no quaking. The battalion commander, Lieutenant Colonel Joseph Zimmer, feared it may have been some kind of sophisticated ruse to get the joint task force to abandon their defensive positions. It was possible their communications and surveillance systems had been hacked, and the information received on the ICBM attack was false, all in an attempt to infiltrate the area and take control. The lieutenant colonel radioed up to the Communication and Surveillance Control Center (CSCC), formerly the HDPD security office headquarters, for a situational report (sitrep) on activity from the visual surveillance system on the dam. Discovering there was no movement in or around the dam and reservoir, the lieutenant colonel then ordered their communications officer to contact Garrison Headquarters, Boulder City and Nellis AFB, Las Vegas for sitreps. There was no response from either. Zimmer then ordered Logan to send two squads topside to verify that there indeed was no activity on or around the dam. Sergeant Danvers took one squad to the Arizona side, while Sergeant Calhoun took his squad to the Nevada side of the dam. When both sergeants were on station, meaning they were in position and prepared to execute operations, Logan told them to execute, and both squads did a simultaneous insertion to the outside. Except, there would be no sitreps coming from either squad leader. Being surveilled from the CSCC, what they saw happen to the soldiers once they got outside was nearly indescribable. From their monitors, they witnessed both squads melting, literally.

As the CSCC was giving report, it was interrupted by horrid, anguished screams. Logan was certain someone cried, "Help us, we're melting," before the radio went silent, but the pained cry had been garbled. Zimmer was standing next to Logan and Benny. He snatched the radio from Logan and attempted to make contact, but no reply was given. He then ordered Logan to send a squad to the CSCC to see what had happened. Logan advised against it, but Zimmer told him there would be hell to pay if he disobeyed a direct order. Logan complied. He sent a corporal to lead another squad. Their sitrep was only filled with tortured screams. Lt Col Zimmer ordered Logan to send Sfc Lee and the remainder of D platoon to the CSCC. Thirty-eight soldiers had now lost their lives. Logan wasn't about to sacrifice anymore.

Every senior field-grade commander is not asked to surrender all independent moral judgment when they sign their enlistment papers. Logan's obligation was to defend The Republic Constitution and safe-guard the welfare of his subordinates. Implicit is the obligation to challenge a commanding officer's orders whose consequences threaten either without apparent good reason.

"With all due respect, Colonel, that order is palpably immoral and illegal. And I refuse to obey it on the grounds you are knowingly and needlessly sending more troops to their deaths, which will cause further military disaster."

"Sergeant Lee, I order you to arrest First Sergeant Ross for insubordination," Zimmer commanded.

"To comply with that order, sir, is to be complicit in murder," Lee told him. "I decline."

Zimmer tried to pull his pistol, but Lee stopped him. Then Zimmer's command staff attempted to enforce the lieutenant colonel's order but that didn't go so well for the two captains and two majors. Those loyal to Logan and Benny saw to it.

"You'll both be court-martialed for this," Zimmer warned.

Logan returned, "I certainly hope I live long enough for that little pleasure, Colonel." Logan then turned to the rest of the soldiers in the room. "Any of you disagree with my command decision and would like to follow the colonel's orders by committing suicide, feel free to volunteer to see what happened in the CSCC." No one volunteered. "All right then. As the highest-ranking NCO and your platoon commander, I am assuming command until further notice. Does anyone disagree with that?" No one disagreed. "Very good. Lieutenant Gibbons," he called to the second lieutenant, who was in charge of the Corps of Engineers platoon.

John Gibbons quickly made his way to Logan. "Yes, First Sergeant Ross."

Logan instructed the junior officer, "Take a detail and some dam personnel, and go shut down the ventilation system—and anything else that could potentially let in whatever is out there." Logan then told the troops inside the room, "Men. Women. Third gender. We'll hunker down for 72 hours, then I'll go topside to make sure it's clear," he announced, and then turned to Zimmer. "That satisfy you, sir?" he asked the lieutenant colonel. "Benny, take Colonel Zimmer and his staff to the turbine repair shop and lock them in; then post two guards."

Forty-two hours into Logan's mandated waiting period, Benny was getting a bit antsy. He was fidgety and couldn't sit still. Benny began to pace back and forth across the long room, making others huddled inside apprehensive as well.

"Benny," Logan called. "Give the pucker valve a rest. Come here and sit down," Logan gestured to a spot next to him. Benny sat as requested. "Thirty more hours, that's all," Logan assured him. "Then we'll be back topside, doing what we always do."

"And what is that?"

Logan smiled and said, "Nothin'."

Logan's jest didn't ease Benny's anxiety. "I don't like this," Benny told him. "Don't like it at all. At least when we were waiting to push forward, we knew what we'd be fighting against. This. Whatever it is. This isn't good," Benny fretted. He then added, "Damn it. At least if I had my violin, I'd have something to do."

"We've gone through a lot of shit, brother, and we've always pulled through. We'll get through this, too. My word."

Benny looked at Logan and asked, "How are you so calm?"

"I have to be," he told Benny as he rolled a handmade bracelet around his wrist. He looked to Benny and finished, "For everyone else's sake. I have to be."

Benny saw Logan nervously playing with the wristlet. He questioned, "Is that the bracelet that the Miranda girl gave you just as we left for boot camp? What was her first name?"

"Jessica," he fondly said. "Jessica Miranda."

"Yeah, Jessica. She's the girl that kicked Gino Madanello in the nuts for picking on you in 9th grade, right?"

"Same girl."

"Geez, I remember that. She was like eleven. She came over from the middle school building halfway through the semester. Came right into the lunch room. Tapped Gino on the shoulder and when he turned around—*Bam!* She kicked that douche nozzle square in the nutsack with those combat boots she had on, and then head butted him in the nose. He went down clutching his balls, gasping for air, tears and blood rolling down his face. The whole lunch room broke out in cheers and laughter. That was probably the best day of 9th grade. Probably all of high school," Benny affectionately reminisced. "She had such a crush on you, didn't she?"

Logan didn't say anything, but his smile confirmed she did.

Benny continued, "And you've had that bracelet on since she gave it to you?"

"Mostly. Had to take it off during boot camp. But after that…"

"So, you did like her?"

"She was my neighbor. We shared the same bus shelter together. She was a kid. Thirteen when we left."

"Hell, Logan. We were kids, too, have you forgotten? Seventeen, a week out of junior year, when we enlisted… You never did tell me what she whispered in your ear before she planted that lip smack on you."

"That's right, I didn't."

Benny waited a moment, hoping Logan would finally reveal his secret. Logan didn't say a word.

"Oh, that's how it is?" Benny said, a bit disappointed. "After all these years. Not even with your best friend, huh? The bracelet. The kiss. The secret whisper you won't talk about. Says a lot," Benny said, nodding knowingly.

Benny was correct. He did care for Jessica. She and Logan had known each other as neighbors all their lives. Jessica's parents owned the property almost directly across the road from him. The Mirandas were egg farmers, and the Ross family grew hay. However, this was not the main source of the Ross family income. Logan's father was half owner of Hogan Ross & Jim Reynolds Inc., a feed mill and farm supply retail store.

Logan had never spoken to Jessica until her first day in 6th grade, when Jessica started coming to the bus shelter to wait for the bus to take her to middle school, which was attached the high school. Logan found her oddly fascinating and weirdly attractive. She was a bit plump for her height and already had developed big boobs, at least larger than normal for a girl her age. She had spikey short black hair that she cut and dyed herself. Jessica liked to wear torn, black jeans that were too small for her. She also wore t-shirts with odd phrases emblazoned on them, like "Did I ask you?" "Me? Weird? Always." "Shhhhh No One Cares." "Cute But Psycho." "The Disneyland Is Calling And I Must Go." Over her shirts she always wore her favorite retro reproduction hoodie from the oldies band OneRepublic. Or on occasion another oldies band called Fall Out Boy. Accentuating her clothing ensemble, she always wore brightly colored socks pulled high on her pant legs, so they showed above the collar of her black combat boots. Whatever Jessica's eclectic style was, it always looked good on her. Everything about her was appealing to him. Logan often told her he liked what she was wearing, hoping to break the ice between them, but she never spoke back. Not until two and a half months into the school year. Logan was sitting with her under the shelter during a rainy morning. The gloom of the day was bringing him down a bit, so he decided to open up his backpack and take out his lunch bag. From it, Logan retrieved six chocolate Teardrops. They were called Teardrops because the bite-sized pieces of chocolate were shaped like a teardrop and wrapped in light-blue colored, lightweight aluminum foil. He offered her one. Jessica waved him off at first. Logan tried a second time. "They're not going to kill you. Unless you're a diabetic. Are you?" he questioned. Jessica shook her head no. Logan asked, "You don't like chocolate?" Jessica still refused to speak to him. "I'm sorry I'm not cool enough for you to talk to. Though, talking isn't required when you're sucking on a Teardrop." Logan gestured with his open hand again, hoping to coax her into taking one. Jessica looked at the chocolates, then at Logan, and then back down to Logan's open hand. "It's okay. I won't miss a few. I have more at home."

Jessica looked up to Logan, and softly said, "I'm not allowed."

"Not allowed?" Logan question. "Not allowed to talk or not allowed to have chocolate?"

"Chocolate," Jessica confessed. "My mother doesn't allow it. Sugar is bad for you, she says."

"Sure," Logan agreed. "If you shove it in your piehole every day." Logan looked around, checking to see if anyone was spying on them, and then said, "Guess what? I don't see your mother. Live life to its fullest. Have a piece of the best chocolate ever invented. It'll bring you to joyous tears. The reason they're called Teardrops." Logan held out his hand again and encouraged, "C'mon. Be a rebel. I promise not to tell."

Jessica tentatively took the confection from Logan's hand. She timidly said, "Thank you."

Unwrapping it she popped it in her mouth and let it melt on her tongue. Jessica's face lit with a wondrous smile. She shook her head agreeingly and said, "Cool."

That was the beginning of their friendship. Every Friday Logan brought Teardrops to the bus shelter and shared them with her. Sometimes he would play guitar and sing her songs that his band was learning or that he learned for himself. Logan even went so far as to learn the OneRepublic song "Apologize," which admittedly was a bit out of Logan's vocal range.

Jessica eventually learned to trust Logan and let herself be a bit vulnerable, though their conversations still remained reserved. That was until the day he and Benny were about to get into the Lee family pickup truck to go to the Territorial Guard base in Walton, NY. Jessica came from across the street to say goodbye and brought Logan a gift. She had made him a beaded rope bracelet. Giving it to him, she whispered, "I love you. When you come back, I want you to be my first." As a final gesture, she gave Logan a big kiss on the lips, though it had been on Logan's face covering. Logan was stunned, both by her confession and by the kiss. He didn't know what to say. He just kept staring at her with a dumbfounded look as the pickup pulled down the driveway. They both watched each other as the truck left the property. Following, Jessica ran out to the street and she remained there until the pickup was too far down the road for Logan to see her anymore. All along Benny kept asking him what Jessica had whispered, but Logan refused to tell him.

Unquestionably, he and Jessica were friends. He had a bond with her. He missed her. Jessica had a way about her that could always get him to smile or laugh. He had barely laughed or smiled since he enlisted. There was also an infatuation on his part. She was cute, funny, smart, and best of all, a little weird. He wasn't sure if it had just been a schoolboy crush or if he was in love with her. It didn't matter. They both had been kids, though she was almost five years younger than he. It would have been inappropriate to pursue a romantic relationship.

He had thought Benny had forgotten by now, but he hadn't. If Jessica hadn't meant as much to him as she did, he probably would have boasted about her proposition moments after it had happened. Then again probably not. Something like that getting around could mark any young girl as a slut. He wasn't one of those fucktard boys, who found it amusing to start vicious rumors about girls and their virtue, or lack of it. He was raised to be a gentleman.

Logan's face lit with a slight smile as he reminisced.

Benny poked him, and said, "You're thinking about her now, aren't you?"

Logan gave him a half-truth. "Nope. Thinking about Teardrops."

"Teardrops?!" he replied, astounded. "You mean that chocolate you used to carry around? Man, if you're thinking about candy instead of a woman, you need therapy."

"And what about your crush, Benny? You know. Laurie Irving. You never told me what happened after she moved," Logan reminded him.

"Laurie. Don't want to talk about her."

"Goes both ways, buddy," Logan prodded him as he stood up. "Going to check on the troops and then go down to the turbine floor to piss. Try not to freak everyone out while I'm gone," Logan jokingly told him.

Laurie Irving. Benny hadn't thought about her since 10th grade. He had fallen in love with her the first day of Kindergarten class, and by the time First Grade was over, Laurie had given him a peck on the cheek. It was the greatest moment in the entirety of elementary school. His love for her lasted through the 10th grade, a year after she moved to Albany, NY. Her leaving broke his heart. Her finding a boyfriend in her new school was like he'd been torn apart and put back together with a couple of pieces in wrong.

"Maybe I'm the one that needs therapy," Benny whispered.

———

As promised, Logan headed topside to see if it was safe for the troops to return to their posts. He relinquished command to 2Lt Gibbons, and requested that the command staff remain in lockup until he came back or was dead. Quietly, Logan told Benny to make sure that happened but also told him not to go too hard on the junior officer.

Logan had taken the employee elevator up to the CSCC. The entire hallway leading to it and the room itself was a mess with liquefied chunky remains that were flecked in fluorescent yellow. It was slow going as he attempted not to step in any of the goo. The stench was so horrendous it was more of a fetid taste than a smell. Logan radioed back his findings, and told the second lieutenant and Benny he hadn't melted and felt fine. Whatever had seeped into the CSCC level appeared to have dissipated.

Stepping out onto the roadway of the dam, Logan removed his full face respirator mask, took a deep breath, and waited. He stood in the daylight for a few minutes before 2Lt Gibbons' radio calls forced him to report in.

"We're clear up here. No enemy sighted and no melting flesh. At your command, Lieutenant, security force can re-deploy." Logan reported.

Within ten minutes troops were coming topside and going back to their duty stations. The Corps of Engineers reopened the ventilation system, and then proceeded to do a complete system diagnostic of the power complex. Gibbons left the command staff in lockup for the time being. He wanted Logan and Benny to take two squads into Boulder City and Nellis AFB to investigate why both were unresponsive. Gibbons was certain that if he released the colonel before he sent 1Sg Ross and Sfc Lee on the mission, the colonel would just arrest the two, and probably him too, the moment the command staff were released.

Gibbons implicitly trusted the two of them to get the mission done. However, Logan thought it ill-advised to order any soldier into the away mission. It may have been safe on the dam, but no one could assure it was also safe in Boulder City or at Nellis AFB, especially since they had lost communications with the garrison and air base. Logan also suggested that Benny remain behind, just in case. If anything happened to Logan, Benny was more than capable of leading the security force.

Sergeant Marc Romano from Logan's original brigade was the first to volunteer. He was also a friend of Logan and Benny from school. They had first met in automobile technology class together. Ten more quickly followed Marc's lead, including Sergeant David George. David had met Benny and Logan in 6th grade general music class. In 10th grade, the three of them along with David Katzby, another middle school friend, formed a roots rock band. They first called themselves The Great Katzbys, except no one got the pun. So, Benny came up with a new name, The Bruce Lees, since they all loved martial artist and film actor Bruce Lee. Apparently, people still remembered Lee but not the novel *The Great Gatsby*. Benny played violin and keyboard, Logan played guitar and harmonica, David George was the drummer, and David Katzby was the bassist, the main singer, and the mandolin player. David Katzby didn't enlist in the military because at the time he had contracted the virus and was in hospital.

The squad took two tactical combat vehicles. Logan rode in the lead Heavy Guns Carrier (HGC), which had four seats and a shielded heavy machine gun station on the roof, while the rest of the team rode in an eight-wheeled ARTEC Puma II Infantry Fighting Vehicle (IFV). They headed down the Hoover Dam Access Road, and when they got to the U-bend that was partly under the Mike O'Callaghan–Pat Tillman Memorial Bridge—the arch bridge that bypassed the dam—they found the missing Garrison Command convoy. The roadway was a mess. A couple of the heavier transport vehicles had crashed through the low, decorative stone wall that was in place to prevent a regular vehicle from careening over the cliff and into the Colorado River. There had been multiple breach points. One truck had gone through the wall and collided into a bridge pylon. Another had smashed through and over-turned. By the damage to the top of the cliff, it appeared a third truck had crashed through and gone over the overhang. Using the HGC, they had to push a couple of the lighter vehicles out of the way so they could get by.

Garrison Command was on the outskirts of the far side of the city. The Territorial Republic Army had appropriated the Boulder City Municipal Airport and the surrounding area. Though the airport had a short runway, it still could accommodate a variety of vertical and/or short take-off and landing (V/STOL) aircraft. This meant troops and most supplies could be flown directly to the garrison, instead of being flown to Nellis AFB and then ground transported to Boulder City.

There had been few deserted vehicles on the roadway leading from the town toward the dam. Most knew that the escape route out of the city in case of enemy attack was taking Route UT-95 toward Search-light, NV, and continuing onto the Nevada-California border. Of the thoroughfares they took to their destination, they discovered no one living nor any globby remains of the city's residents. The abandoned city gave Logan and his soldiers an uneasy feeling. When they arrived at the garrison, everything was intact. Logan gave a sitrep on their investigation. He reported what had happened to the garrison personnel they had found on the road, and that it appeared no one had stayed behind at the base. Unable to establish contact with Nellis AFB, Logan told 2Lt Gibbons they were continuing on to Nellis, and would give another sitrep after they arrived.

There was a myriad of deserted automobiles and trucks along their route through Las Vegas to the airbase. There had clearly been a panicked exodus by many civilians attempting to flee the area in hopes of not being incinerated by the reported nuke. There was some serpentine maneuvering around vehicles and taking alternate routes. What should have been a forty-minute trip, turned out to be nearly two hours.

Nellis AFB was as deserted as the Ari-Cal-Nev Hoover Dam Joint Task Force Garrison had been. From their investigation it appeared that most of the airbase aviators, and presumably their crews, had evacuated. Logan and his team only found one occupied hangar containing two aircraft, and it was clearly evident by their disassembled state that they were undergoing repair and maintenance. Even with all the pilots and their crews gone, it didn't account for a majority of the bases' personnel. One of the major tenants of the base had been the former UT Air Force Warfare Center, which reported directly to the Air Combat Command, headquartered at Langley Air Force Base, Joint Base Langley–Eustis, Virginia. Since the Nevada Territory had allied with The Republic at the start of the war, the base's Air Force Warfare Center had become the Territorial Republic Air Combat Command (TRACC). The unit accounted for a significant number of the base's command, support and sustainment staff.

Nellis certainly had its secrets, like Areas 6, 52, and 53. However, there was no hidden nuclear bunker deep under the base. That wasn't to say there wasn't an underground level to the air base. The TRACC had a backup command center level concealed under the basement that was there in case main operations suffered a catastrophic event. Included, there were temporary emergency shelters for base personnel. It was all powered by generators that were housed within a Faraday shield room to ensure there was no power failure in case of an EMP attack. This information was public knowledge. The undisclosed part of the backup facility was its location, and it wasn't directly under the TRACC building.

After reporting in, Logan left the runway area and his team headed to TRACC. The building was deserted, as Logan had suspected it would be. They continued through the facility but found no one until they came to a set of elevators. Logan had been correct; it appeared base personnel had remained behind. In the hallway, they found two security force personnel—liquified. Logan called for the elevator. Inside the first car there were six more globby remains of security soldiers. When the other elevator arrived, it too was filled with liquified bodies.

Logan wasn't about to step into an elevator car filled full of decaying human matter. Like at the dam, for all he knew whatever contaminate had caused so much death could still be active in the gooey remains. He also couldn't pick up any security card that might have worked on the nearby stairwell. Even the two cards from the two personnel in the hallway were sitting in a puddle of muck. Logan radioed base to report his findings and ask if Gibbons wanted further investigation or for them to move on to the lower dams. There was no response. After a few attempts, Logan thought it was possible that they were in a communication dead zone. Moving outside, he still could not raise anyone at the dam. Alarmed, Logan and his team sped back to base.

Racing up the Great Basin Highway and about to enter onto the Boulder Dam Access Road, Logan and his team were confronted by two oncoming military trucks that were in the center of the road. The two speeding vehicles forced Logan's driver, Sergeant David George, to jog left onto the sloped dirt embankment just as the two trucks passed. The vehicles made a quick left turn at the T-junction for the viaduct. The vehicles were heading in the direction of route UT-93, which would take them around Boulder City. Luckily, Logan's follow vehicle hadn't been too close behind, for it too had to make a quick jog left to avoid a collision with the oncoming vehicles.

When the team arrived back to the dam, there were no soldiers crewing their positions, no vehicles either. Logan knew something bad had happened to make everyone flee. He kept radioing Benny and 2Lt Gibbons. Still neither responded. Logan and his team headed inside. When the elevator arrived, there were two dead soldiers inside. Their corpses were not melted, but rather riddled with bullet holes. In the hallway leading to the gold room, there were more bodies. All had been shot in the back. As they cautiously continued on, they found Lt Col Zimmer dead across the threshold. A few feet inside was 2Lt John Gibbons, who had a suffered a fatal neck wound. The room looked like a warzone. The walls were riddled with bullet holes and there were corpses of a dozen warfighters on the floor.

Logan knew if Benny was not amongst the dead then he had to be somewhere within the dam structure. He would have never abandoned his duty as a warfighter. Their continued search led the team to the turbine maintenance floor, which was under the turbine level. It was where Benny had taken the colonel and his staff. The room where Zimmer and his cronies had been held wasn't occupied. They continued on, coming to a janitorial services room. When Sergeant Marc Romano cautiously reached over and turned the handle, a rapid succession of bullets ripped through the door at them.

"Stand down, stand down" Logan called out and then identified himself. "This is First Sergeant Ross. I'm looking for Sergeant Lee."

"Sergeant Lee?" a voice answered from behind the door. "Yeah, I got him."

"Who am I speaking to?

"CW2 Crncevic, Army Corps of Engineers."

"Well, Chief Crncevic. What do I need to do to get him back?"

Crncevic said, "Nothing, if it's really you. Except slipping your ID under the door to prove it's actually you."

Logan removed his ID badge from its protective sleeve that was strapped around his upper arm, and quickly slipped it under the door.

Crncevic called out, "First Sergeant Ross. I'm going to unlock the door and surrender my weapon. Your word as a soldier you won't shoot," the soldier requested.

Logan returned, "No one is going to shoot as long as you don't."

The door unlocked, and then swung open. A soldier in his early 30s was standing with his hands on his head and his pistol at his feet.

"Kick your weapon to us, Chief," Logan ordered.

The chief warrant officer told him, "Sergeant Lee is hurt, First Sergeant."

Sergeants Romano and George pulled Crncevic clear of the doorway and detained him.

"What happened?" Logan demanded to know, as he went to check on his friend.

"It was Colonel Zimmer," Crncevic began.

Second Lieutenant John Gibbons had let the colonel and staff out of detention, and had them brought to the gold room moments after Logan and his team had departed. Zimmer was privy to Logan's sitrep of Garrison Command, and Gibbons' instructions to check out Nellis' TRACC building. After Logan gave his first sitrep in regard to the runway and hangar area, LT COL Zimmer and his staff made their move to retake control. Gibbons had let his guard down, never thinking the colonel would make such a bold and risky move. Zimmer took advantage of it with a simultaneous takeover. Major Mignone grabbed for Gibbons' pistol, as the other three staff officers and Zimmer grabbed for weapons from the nearest soldiers. A longer than expected struggle happened between a private and the colonel, who was trying to wrestle the carbine free from the subordinate. Somehow the safety switch was moved into firing position. The assault weapon began to fire wildly as the two struggled to gain control of it. Bullets pelted the walls and the ceiling, including striking soldiers. Once that happened, the room came ablaze with gunfire. In the midst of the melee, Gibbons had been shot in the throat. Clutching his wound, hoping to hold back the blood flow, he ended up collapsing against a wall.

Benny had been on the opposite end of the room speaking to a Corps of Engineers warrant officer and one of the civilian engineers when the fracas broke out. They were updating Benny on the diagnostic of the power house, which had just been completed. Benny was shot in the chest from a stray bullet. The impact to his body armor knocked him off his feet. He hit his head on the floor after collapsing.

The civilian next to Benny took one to the head. CW2 Milan Crncevic was unscathed. He grabbed Benny and pulled him out the door. Other soldiers fled behind them, and ended up knocking Crncevic down. The tumble had been a stroke of luck, for Lt Col Zimmer had crossed the room and was cutting those down who were attempting to escape. The last thing Crncevic saw was the colonel's forehead exploding from a bullet ripping through it. 2Lt Gibbons was a few feet behind Zimmer with a pistol in his hand. When Gibbons collapsed, Crncevic went to check on him. It was too late, though. When he reached him, Gibbons had bled-out.

As for all the other dam personnel on the base, Crncevic didn't know anything about the situation. After the initial mayhem, he grabbed the unconscious Lee, took him down to the janitor's maintenance room and locked themselves in, hoping Logan would return and find them before someone hostile did. Unfortunately, neither Benny or CW2 Crncevic had a radio with them.

Logan was pretty sure what had happened to the rest of the dam personnel. They simply fled, like the two trucks of personnel that had sped by them. From what Logan and his team had discovered, the countries of the world had not launched a nuclear strike against America; it had been a biological DNA weapons attack. For all intents and purposes, the civil war was over. So, what was next? That's what Logan needed to think about.

The command staff was dead, the dam's defensive positions had been abandoned, the CSCC was a remediation nightmare, and all but one of the civilian staff had fled along with nearly the entire Corps of Engineers. As best as Logan could surmise there was no longer an enemy to fight or a Territorial Republic of America to fight for. Indeed, the war was over. He told his subordinates this, and then informed them that when Benny awoke, Delaware Brigade—now just four of them—was going to pull out and head back to the District of New York. First, they were going to go to the Ari-Cal-Nev Joint Task Force Garrison to load up enough supplies to help get them home. He welcomed the remainder to do the same. If any of them were heading east, he suggested they travel together since they truly had no idea of what awaited them beyond the Las Vegas area.

Benny awoke a few hours later. Logan told him his plan and Benny agreed. Twelve of them left together. After packing up their vehicles, five of the 12 departed with only two riding together. CW2 Crncevic had been stationed in the Corps of Engineers Pacific Division - Arizona Field Office in Phoenix, when the Arizona Territory joined The Republic. He was divorced and his ex-wife still lived in Riverside, CA, where he once had been stationed. Though the divorce had mostly been amicable, he had no ties with his former wife since. As for his parents, they had emigrated from Serbia and had both passed away over six years ago and a few months apart from one another. There was no one in his life and no reason to return to Phoenix, unless it was to retrieve a few cherished personal items. He asked Logan if he could join his team on their quest to return home. Logan was glad to have him.

Logan, Benny, Marc, David, and Milan would wait until the following morning to leave. Since the garrison had a large communications center, they tried to reach any Republic command stations that might still be operational. After two hours of trying, they realized it was futile. Logan wanted to map out a route that would take them through known Republic Territories and where he was aware there had been Forward Operating and/or Fire Bases. He knew they would have to refuel and restock supplies along the way. It was going to be a challenging and long journey home.

The group tried to get some sleep that night but found they couldn't. Since they were all behind the wire of the garrison's perimeter fencing, only one guard was posted near their encampment with everyone taking four hours shifts. Marc was on first watch.

Logan was sitting under a cloudy sky near a fire he had made inside a used metal drum. The fire wasn't for the warmth of the heat it radiated; it was for ambience. Logan had his acoustic guitar with him and if there was anything that could relieve his anxiety it was playing music. The moment he started performing "Ripple" by the Grateful Dead, it didn't take but a few minutes for the rest of the team to start making their ways to him.

Milan and David were the first to gather around. When Benny heard Logan and David singing Bob Dylan's "You Ain't Goin' Nowhere," Benny finally decided to get out of bed. When the song was finished, Benny questioned Logan, "You salvaged your guitar? Thought it got crushed in the rubble." Referring to the damaged Mercantile Building.

Logan flipped his guitar over and showed Benny the back. It had a hole that had been inelegantly repaired. "Cardboard and duct tape, brother. Now aren't you glad you left that $8,000 violin of yours at home?" Logan turned to David George and said, "Okay, Sticks, how about laying down some beats?" Sticks was David's band nickname. Partly because he was a drummer, and the rest because he was six foot tall and lanky. As soon as Logan began picking the strings, David knew immediately it was "Bron-Y-Aur Stomp" by Led Zeppelin. Zeppelin, as they were called by their fans, was one of David's favorite Classic Rock bands. "Bron-Y-Aur Stomp" was also a song David sang lead vocals on. This was not a song in the repertoire of the Bruce Lees, it was a song that David, Benny, and Logan had learned for fun. They used to perform it around the campfire at the cabin Marc Romano's family used to rent during the summer in Roscoe, NY. While David kept rhythm by slapping on an empty supply crate he was seated on, like it was a Cajón percussion instrument, Benny added the hand claps.

The music lasted a few more hours until it was Logan's turn for watch. When Logan got up, he walked over to the blazing drum, and then chucked his guitar into it. Everyone was shocked at the act, especially Benny. "Holy shit biscuits. What was that for?"

With a big grin, Logan returned, "Back to the barn."

Milan was more confused with Logan's statement, but David and Benny understood. The barn was at the Ross homestead—the place where the Bruce Lees rehearsed—where Logan had left the guitars he cherished most.

PART II

GOIN' HOME

ALTHOUGH THE HEAVY GUNS CARRIER (HGC) AND THE PUMA II relied on nearly antiquated fossil fuel, Logan kept them because both had maximum road speeds of 70 mph and were excellent fighting vehicles. Land forces were still well behind in using current energy sources when compared to other branches of the military, or even civilian use. All mid- to heavy-sized military vehicles still used diesel, as did civilian transportation trucks. Whereas, submarines used cold fusion reactors, ships—both military and commercial—used a specialized catalytic converter that transformed carbon dioxide and hydrogen from seawater into a liquid hydrocarbon fuel. Civilian vehicles relied mainly on hydrogen. Hydrogen vehicles were basically electric cars with a fuel tank. They boasted the performance and instant torque of battery electric cars, while providing greater range than any pure electric vehicle, and obviating range anxiety and lengthy charging stops. Plus, hydrogen was the most abundant element in the universe. There were still some car enthusiasts that still held onto their old electric cars and their antique fossil fuel classic vehicles.

Notwithstanding the two fighting vehicles' shortcomings concerning their horrible carbon foot print, there were also practical and tactical reasons for Logan choosing to take the Puma II and the HGC. The Puma could carry six troops, plus a driver, a gunner, and a commander. Albeit there was no sleeping compartment, there was actually a built-in toilet under one of the forward seats of the mission module. However, the toilet wasn't the reason Logan took the eight-wheeled vehicle. Unlike the HGC which had been produced in the United Territories, and was seized when the Republic was founded, the Puma II had been purchased by The Republic from ARTEC GmbH in Munich, Germany. The Puma II was superior to the enemy's Cobra III eight-wheeled armored fighting vehicle in that its protection against mines and ballistic threats reached new standards. It also had a high-level of protection under extreme climatic conditions and in engagements with the enemy. Unfortunately, the one that Logan and his team were using didn't come equipped with a Rheinmetall LANCE II two-man turret with a 30mm caliber machine cannon and a secondary machine gun. Many Pumas were not equipped with any type of fully automated remote weapon station because of The Republic's lack of money.

Only one platoon—seven Pumas and their crews—had been assigned to the garrison from the 81st Brigade Combat Team, which consisted of mainly eight-wheeled Cobra III combat vehicles that were acquired when California joined The Republic. The vehicles that were at the garrison instead had manual shielded heavy machine gun stations on the roof with Sig Sauer's PM338, a six-barrel rotary machine gun with a high rate of fire using .338 Norma Magnum ammunition. The PM was the abbreviation for Patriot Minigun or simply the "Patriot". Sig Sauer was the main firearms and ammunition supplier for The Republic, being headquartered in New Hampshire in the New England Colonial Territory. They also supplied the standard issued individual assault rifle, which was the MCX Spear Mod 4 chambered in 6.8mm with quick-detach suppressor, and a 30-round detachable box magazine.

Next to it was a commander's hatch. The vehicle also had four observation/gunner hatches on the mission module. The only accessory item of note was an extended external storage rack mounted above the hydraulic rear door. This added feature was a plus since the Puma's interior storage could only hold 96 hours of combat supplies. The HGC, however, had the ability to tow a two-wheeled trailer. With a trailer full of Combat Cloth Face Coverings (CCFC), food, pistol, machine gun and rifle ammunition, a box of fragmentation grenades, a case of Claymore anti-personnel mines, some medical supplies, spare clothing and boots, and some backup weaponry, the two-vehicle convoy headed to Phoenix. Taking Crncevic with them was the least Delaware Platoon could do for the man that saved Benny's life.

It indeed had been a long journey to the east. In their travels they discovered that the DNA bombs did not wipe out all of humanity. There were survivors, which they avoided. Logan was concerned there may be enemy units that were still determined to fight. Most of the country's middle territories were part of the UTA. There was no way to avoid crossing through at least one UTA territory. Logan decided to head north to cross the UTA's Nebraska Territory and into The Republic's Iowa Territory, then east to the Middle Colonial Territory. Iowa was not a territory that Logan, Benny, Marc or David were fondly looking forward to re-visiting. However, there wasn't much of a choice. There was a large forward operating base at Dubuque. The base would hopefully still have some much-needed fuel and some add-on food. Hopefully, they could get the base partly operational again and be able to take a hot shower. That would be a luxury for them. If the base was still viable, they could layover awhile. But it was Dubuque, and the great battle they all had fought in held horrible memories.

Once part of the Middle Colonial Territorial National Guard Reserve, the Delaware Company was absorbed into the Army of the Territorial Republic of America to replace losses during the Battle of Mount Morris along the Pennsylvania border. As the war progressed, Logan's company got smaller and kept being reassigned to different brigades; eventually what remained ended up in a Puma Brigade Combat Team (PBCT) guarding the southern border of the Michigan Territory. Then came the enemy invasion of the Iowa Territory.

The UTA had launched a massive offensive to capture Iowa, and it had been mostly successful. They were pushing hard toward Dubuque. It would be a strategic loss for The Republic if captured. If the enemy controlled the city, they would control the two passenger and railroad bridges that crossed over the Mississippi River and into the southern end of the Wisconsin Territory. The UTA could then launch a campaign to capture southern Wisconsin by simultaneously invading it from the west and the south from their border city of Savanna, Illinois.

As part of The Republic's counter defense, one battalion of Logan's PBCT was being deployed to southern Wisconsin. Three of the five companies that made up the battalion were being sent to enhance defensive positions along the southern border. Logan's company, along with another, would be deployed to Forward Operating Base (FOB) Julien—formerly the Iowa National Guard Ready Center—in Iowa

City to help defend the Dubuque area, its bridges, and to make sure the base didn't fall into enemy hands.

The Dubuque Regional Airport didn't have runways long enough to accommodate the large military transport aircraft that were required to get the PBCT into theatre. The closest airport that could be used was the Dane County Regional Airport, which was a civil-military airport located six miles northeast of downtown Madison, the capital of Wisconsin. Deploying from the Battle Creek Air Base, the battalion landed in Madison, 76 hours after they received their orders.

All minor passenger vehicle bridges to the south over the Mississippi River that connected Iowa to Illinois had been destroyed. The few major crossings were defensively reinforced to prevent the UTA from using them. However, this didn't stop the UTA from getting troops from the Southeast into the territory. As part of their strategy, they had air dropped a large contingent of equipment and troops into Bellevue, IA, and began a northern push toward Dubuque. By the time Logan's battalion reached East Dubuque WI, enemy forces had captured the Julien Dubuque Bridge and had established an offensive head along the shoreline. The enemy was battering East Dubuque to soften The Republic's position in preparation of an invasion. Intelligence reports from the 128th Air Control Squadron reported that after UTA land armies captured the territorial capitol of Des Moines, they went northeast instead of east to FOB Julien in Iowa City. The enemy had decided not to engage FOB Julien. They also did not invade Waterloo but continued east until Dyersville, where half of their forces then headed north to Luxemburg as the remainder continued toward Dubuque. It was evident that the northern UTA forces were planning to continue to the Mississippi, and then head south in order to capture the Dubuque-Wisconsin Bridge. With forces coming in three directions, the UTA could easily capture the city.

Quick Reaction Force troops from FOB Julien had been dispatched and had intercepted the eastbound UTA forces at Farley, IA that were heading for Dubuque. Though The Republic hadn't destroyed the enemy or made them retreat, they had halted the enemy's advance. Meanwhile, The Republic's 115th Fighter Wing was engaged on two fronts doing guided bombing while also engaging the enemy in air-to-air combat. The 115th was attempting to slow the enemy's progress so that the combined forces of the PBCT and the one infantry and one field artillery battalions from the Wisconsin Infantry Brigade Combat Team (Mechanized) could mount a counter offensive before the enemy surrounded Dubuque. Complicating The Republic's situation, they could no longer use the Highway 61/Dubuque-Wisconsin Bridge that was three miles north. Once the news reached the bridge station commander that the enemy was coming from the north, coupled with the fall and loss of the command staff at the Julien Dubuque Bridge, the commanding lieutenant panicked. Without orders from his superiors at FOB Julien, he ordered the demolition of the bridge along the shoreline as his unit retreated across the Mississippi into Wisconsin.

The two PBCT companies entered Fire Support Base Albert—named after Albert Sale, a soldier in the U.S. Army who served with 8th U.S. Cavalry in the Arizona Territory during the Apache Wars—an hour after UTA began its battery of the city. The enemy had already crippled most of The Republic's field artillery and killed a third of the infantry battalion, including its commanding officer. Upon disembarking, Colonel Julie Holt, Logan's commanding officer, took charge of the forces and ordered what was left of the artillery to concentrate their efforts on eliminating the enemy's shoreline positions. Col Holt was determined to launch a counter-offensive and crossover to Dubuque and route the enemy. Nevertheless, the UTA had their own battle plans. The Puma II column didn't make it halfway over the bridge when they encountered superior resistance, which forced them to retreat after suffering the loss of five vehicles and 43 troops. Holt was planning on a second push but needed another wave of air support. Planning with the command staff, an artillery major told Holt about an old railroad tunnel that was out of enemy sight, due to it being bored under a 150-foot bluff very close to the Mississippi riverbank. It was being used to store munitions. If the Puma II vehicles could navigate the East Dubuque Railroad Tunnel, it would deliver them at the head of the Dubuque Railroad Bridge. If the colonel was willing to send his Pumas and the infantry across the 1,260-foot-long, steel deck through-truss bridge, they might be able to rout the enemy and gain back the Julien Dubuque crossing. It was risky. If the enemy discovered the mobilization across the narrow, single track bridge, they could easily re-maneuver part of their Cobra vehicles to the bridge exit and halt the advance.

There was also a matter of the tunnel itself. The 851-foot portal to portal tunnel ran at a 90-degree turn underneath the bluff. Although the tunnel was not long, the harsh curve had proven to be an issue for the railroad company, and pre-war was only used a few times a day. Complicating its use further was the fact that it was a single rail tunnel, which meant it was narrow. A common boxcar at its maximum was 9 feet, 6 inches wide. A Puma II was 9 feet, 10 inches wide. The width of the tunnel was barely 12 feet wide. There was no room for navigational error and the Pumas would have to traverse very slowly.

It was a sound strategy. The colonel decided to split her PBCT and the remaining infantry equally. Phase One would be to get the Pumas into the tunnel. Holt knew exactly what operational unit she wanted to lead the East Dubuque Railroad Tunnel mission, and it was Echo Company. Not only did Echo Company have an incredibly talented commander with a proven reputation on the battlefield, it also had Sergeant First Class Logan Ross and his fierce warriors.

Even though Logan had been an enlisted soldier, he showed himself to be an incredibly strategic warfighter, and a master tactician. Where most soldiers have a mediocre rise through the ranks, Logan and his subordinates rose quickly and noticeably. Logan had made his name by being able to adapt and react quickly to a changing battlefield, and to turn the tide of a battle to a Republic advantage. His accomplishments, and those of his unit, had earned them three field promotions, and gotten the attention of not only his immediate commanders but also the attention of the war department and Chief Dennis Scott, leader of The Republic.

Once the lead vehicle was at the mouth of the east portal, phase two would commence. A precision airstrike would be called in to hit the enemy's shoreline batteries. As that was happening, the second attempt to cross the bridge would commence, while simultaneously the crossing of the railway bridge would begin. If everything went according to plan, the enemy would not be able to repel the bridge crossings.

Normally there were 14 Puma vehicles and 180 troops in each company. However, Col Holt had reassigned two vehicles and their crews from Logan's Echo Company to Alpha Company, which had suffered significant loss of firepower on the first attempted crossing. In charge of Logan's Echo Company was Captain William Tomczak. Col Holt, Capt Tomczak, and the captain of Alpha Company coordinated the assault from the fire support base. The railroad strike force was commanded by First Lieutenant Mark Marczak. In turn, each vehicle was commanded by a sergeant. 1Lt Marczak led the charge out of the tunnel and onto the bridge. Marczak's command vehicle was followed by Logan. Sgt Marc Romano was his driver. Benny was in the second to last vehicle of the column. His driver was Sgt David George. Everything went according to plan until Echo Company had reached the three-quarter mark.

The enemy had begun its advance across the Julien Dubuque Bridge with their Cobra vehicle company. They intended to meet The Republic's forces and drive them from the bridge. There had been no intelligence reports that the UTA had any Cobra III Anti-Tank Guided Missile (ATGM) Vehicles with them when they captured the Julien Dubuque Bridge—but they did. Discovering The Republic was moving forward over the river via the railroad bridge, the UTA began a simultaneous assault on both crossings. An enemy Tube-launched, Optically-tracked and Wireless-guided (TOW) missile struck 1LT Marczak's vehicle just under the turret, flipping it on its side, and blowing the vehicle partly against a bridge truss. Then another missile came rocketing at them, destroying the Puma behind Benny's. The enemy had cut off Echo Company's advance and had prevented them from an easy withdrawal. Then a third TOW missile struck the Puma behind Logan. That vehicle had been one of only two Pumas that were equipped with long range anti-tank guided missiles. The other anti-tank missile Puma II was Benny's. With the lieutenant dead, the next highest-ranking soldier was Logan, who was a staff sergeant. Logan ordered the column ahead and for Benny to take out the enemy's Cobra missile vehicle before it took out Benny. Marc Romano pushed at the crippled, burning wreckage in front of them, trying to get it off the bridge. It took a few powerful shoves to get through the narrow opening of one of the truss sections. The command vehicle plummeted 20 feet into the river below. Logan ordered all vehicles equipped with MK30-4/ABM automatic cannons to target the enemy. The Julien Dubuque Bridge was within the maximum effective range of 2.13 miles. Echo Company unleashed a hail of 30mm armor-piercing and high-explosive rounds.

Although both the General Dynamics Cobra III and the ARTEC Puma II eight-wheel combat vehicles had the same baseline integral all-round 16mm protection against machine gun rounds, mortar and artillery fragments, The Republic's vehicles had been purchased with an RPG armor upgrade. Meaning that it could withstand a direct ballistic hit of up to a 40mm caliber round. Benny hit the lead enemy Cobra with the missile launcher and slowed the enemy's advance. Then Logan and the other auto cannon Puma's targeted the front vehicles. As the first follow vehicle went around the destroyed Cobra, Benny launched another missile and blew it to pieces, too. He had temporarily halted the enemy's advance. As the Cobras behind the two burning wrecks began to push the burning vehicles out of the way, they were struck with a barrage of 30mm rounds. A second TOW missile capable Cobra III had made it onto the bridge and was turning its turret toward Benny's Puma II. Benny saw it and quickly locked in the enemy vehicle and fired. Except the enemy's missile launched before Benny's struck the Cobra III ATGM vehicle. Luckily, the TOW missile was a bit antiquated for modern warfare in regard to the enemy's missile operator having to continually point a sighting device at the target while the missile was in flight. Without him the missile didn't strike the Puma II where the enemy had intended. The missile clipped the back of the Puma. In a fiery explosion the backend of the vehicle blew apart and reared up. The troops inside the crew mission module were instantly killed as was Benny's missile operator. However, with the drive module door closed, Benny and David had been protected from the blast. They both escaped the burning wreckage out the command hatch and had made it clear of the blast zone before the ordinance inside detonated, ripping the vehicle apart and creating a multidirectional metal hailstorm.

Logan and the remainder of the column made it across the bridge just as UTA forces had made it to Sageville, which was only nine miles from the 11th Street entry to the destroyed Dubuque-Wisconsin Bridge. Getting off the tracks at an industrial area, Logan split his forces. Benny took command of five Pumas and went toward the Julien Dubuque Bridge, taking with him three-quarters of the infantry to help Alpha Company. Logan took his contingent of vehicles and troops to set up flanks along the UTA's approach. For troops, he took three of the four weapons squads that used the FGM-150B Harpoon anti-tank missile launchers. The Harpoon was a soldier-portable, shoulder-fired anti-tank weapon that was four feet long and weighed about 34 pounds. It used a 140mm warhead. Plus, it had a reusable command launch unit with fire-and-forget technology, meaning the operator could pull the trigger and then take cover, not have to make adjustments to the missile flight after firing. It was fully capable of obliterating any enemy vehicle it hit.

Three hours after Benny and Logan engaged their respective enemy forces, the UTA army was in retreat and forces from FOB Julien were in pursuit. However, both Benny's and Logan's units took heavy losses in vehicle and in human life. For their heroism in leading their attacks, they would eventually get 48 hours rest at FOB Julien. That was after they swept the town for any remaining enemy troops that might be hiding, and after a PBCT company was brought up from the southern Wisconsin border to replace losses. Commendations followed, and shortly thereafter came medals with field rank promotions. Then reassignment to Hoover Dam. Everyone that was left alive from Echo Company was included in the transfer. Logan, Benny, David, and Marc, plus those who were left from the original Delaware Company hoped it would be their last assignment.

The Battle of Dubuque did have one extra memory for Logan, the loss of his virginity. As Logan's team was clearing the northeast quadrant of the city, going from building to building and house to house making sure no enemy combatants were hiding out, they came across a large home off Peru Road that was more isolated than its neighbors. Their investigation of the house was met with hostility from a young, wounded UTA corporal who was holding a mother and her seven-year-old daughter hostage. It was clear by the soldier's agitated state that he was frightened and felt threatened. With a cool head and empathy for his injured enemy, Logan was able to get the corporal to calm down and to surrender without violent escalation.

The grateful divorcee thanked everyone for saving the lives of her and her daughter. She was exceptionally grateful to Logan who had kept his head and quickly deescalated the tense situation without resulting in anyone's death. Joyce Michaels told Logan that he should come back later that evening and she would cook for him. She was sure he hadn't had a home cooked meal in a long time. Logan was grateful for the gesture, and told the petite, red-haired woman that it was doubtful since they still needed to check two more residential areas, and then find a place to set up camp for the evening.

Joyce insisted that Logan's team use her property to make camp, since she had plenty of acreage and the property line at the street had a low rising hill that gave an excellent view of the residential neighborhood across the road. Logan accepted her offer.

Benny's squad had joined Logan's in setting up camp. The mild late-Fall night, the glistening stars, and the night noises were rather soothing for everyone after nearly 48 hours of combat and post-combat duties. Much later that evening, Logan went to check on Joyce and her daughter, and to thank Joyce for her generosity on the use of the property. Their casual conversation ended up turning into an evening of torrid passion. She had sex with him in ways that he had often fantasized about, and a couple of ways that he hadn't even imagined. It certainly hadn't been the romantic fantasy he had envisioned for himself for his first time, but it had certainly been an experience he would never forget.

Every territory had suffered infrastructure damage on both sides. High value targets included railroads, important bridge crossings, and manufacturing facilities, especially manufacturers who made weapons and ammunition. Destroyed bridges caused re-routing. Some of the known Republic military bases along their way that Logan thought they could use to resupply had been cleaned out or destroyed. The team had to scavenge diesel from other sources, which were mainly in cities that were struck by the DNA bombs. Early on, survivors hadn't been bold enough to go into major cities to scavenge. The biggest obstacle though, had been the inclement weather. A large heavy snow storm blanketed northeastern Colorado adding to the two plus feet of snow accumulation already on the ground. The heavy, blowing snowfall didn't just slow their pace; it forced their journey to a crawl. They had no choice but to seek immediate shelter. The closest military base was at Fort Carson, Colorado. Like most military bases in America, there was a photovoltaic system installed, which helped supply power to critical areas. Normally, they would have done an aerial recon by drone to ascertain if the base was uninhabited. The snow prevented that from happening, so they proceeded with great caution, especially since the Colorado Territory had fallen to the UTA a year ago. Being within 10 miles of Colorado Springs, they found the base derelict but still supplied. Fort Carson was a place that the team could hole up in until the storm passed.

Heavy, steady snow fell for three days piling drifts up to six feet deep. Marc, Logan and Benny had experienced deep snow before, having been from the Southern Tier of New York, but a massive accumulation in such a short period of time was something they had never experienced. Crncevic, who had little snow experience on any major scale, called it Snowmageddon. There was no way the team was going to risk travelling until the Spring.

The main entry gate to Fort Carson was open and most of the compound lights were on, along with some of the base's interior lights. The base being lit was not necessarily a sign of occupation but it didn't mean there weren't UTA forces still in control. As they drove deeper into the base, the team was on alert, tending both vehicle's gun stations. The accumulated snow was undisturbed. There weren't even animal tracks. It appeared the base had been abandoned or had suffered the catastrophic effects of the DNA bombs.

After clearing the entire base, which took a few hours, and finding no inhabitants or tell-tale signs of deceased occupants, the team went about taking stock of what provisions and munitions remained. There weren't many munitions. The base's arsenal was pretty well depleted. What remained were six cases of 6.8-millimeter 277 TVCM rounds that were used in enemy RM277-AR Mod 3 squad rifles, but also could be used in their MCX Spear Mod 4 rifles. Additionally, there was a partial case of hand grenades and a couple of boxes of pistol ammunition. Luckily, the enemy left more food than they had munitions.

The forced layover was the first time the team had any down time to get to casually chat with one another. They were in the mess hall eating and listening to Logan layout the maintenance schedule on what needed to be done on their vehicles. When Marc said, "Roger that First Sergeant," in acknowledgement, Logan stopped cleaning his MCX Spear Mod 4 rifle and announced, "How about we suspend the formality of rank while we're here? After all, the war is over and most of us have been friends for years. Is that all right with you Chief Crncevic?"

With seriousness Milan returned, "Well, being that I'm the highest non-commissioned rank amongst the five of us, and you've been ignoring my rank since Ari-Cal-Nev fell, rank doesn't seem to matter with you anyway."

Logan immediately stood, assumed the position of attention, and called out, "Team ATTENTION!" Marc, Benny, and David quickly rose, and all four of them sharply saluted Milan. Logan then began his sincere apology for his grievous disrespect. "Begging Chief Crncevic's pardon. With all due respect I apologize for my misconduct in not showing you the due respect and courtesy of your rank. I wrongly assumed command of this unit and do hereby relinquish such authority. Furthermore, I take full responsibility for the actions of my team for also not recognizing you as the ranking soldier."

Milan ordered, "Prove it, prove it, prove it. Prove to me you are truly sorry for the disrespect."

"I'm at your command, Chief Crncevic. How may I be of service?" Logan asked.

"When we left the Hoover Dam, I forgot to pack my fallopian tubes in my toolkit. I want you to search the maintenance bays here and see if you can locate a box of them."

"Begging your pardon, Chief Crncevic, but I don't know what fallopian tubes look like," Logan told him with sincerity.

Milan was not happy with Logan's response. "First Sergeant Ross. If you can't find me a clearly marked box of fallopian tubes on this base, then you're not the soldier I believe you to be. Now dismissed, First Sergeant Ross."

Logan saluted his commander, and after Crncevic reciprocated, he did a sharp about face, grabbed his gear, and went out in search of what was requested of him. Logan had been gone no more than a minute when Crncevic could no longer maintain a straight face. He burst out in hysterical laughter and nearly fell off his chair.

David asked, "Did we all hear you correctly, Chief Crncevic? Did you say *fallopian tubes?*"

Crncevic still couldn't stop laughing. He smacked his hand on the table a couple of times and then gestured for them to wait a moment for an answer. When Crncevic was finally able to speak, he told the group, "Logan needed his pucker valve loosened a bit. He's so tight in the ass."

Marc, Benny, and David began to laugh at the practical joke Crncevic had just pulled on Logan.

Benny remarked, "Oh, Logan is going to be so pissed when he figures it out."

"*If,* he figures it out," David corrected.

The snow was blinding and the wind was whipping, biting at Logan as he trudged through its deepness across the base to the vehicle maintenance shop, where they had parked their two vehicles inside. Cold and miserable, Logan was nearly three-quarters of the way there when the sudden recollection of what a fallopian tube actually was came to him. "Son-of-shit-biscuit," he cursed. "They are so going to pay for this."

If Chief Crncevic and the rest of the team enjoyed a good practical joke, Logan was happy to reciprocate. That night Logan was on exterior guard duty at the base's gate, doing a midnight to 4:00 a.m. watch. Though the small guard house kept most of the inclement weather out, Logan was still chilled to the bone.

At 3:00 a.m., Logan abandoned his post and went back to their sleeping quarters. Having found an aluminum trash can, Logan entered the bunk area, switched on all the lights, and began banging the lid against the can.

The abrupt awakening alarmed them. At first, they thought they were being rattled out of bed because the base was under threat. They quickly realized that was not the case when Logan announced, "I am not satisfied with the conduct of this unit. Some of you soldiers are under the impression that because the war is over you are not required to wear full BDUs. Well, you're wrong. You're a disgrace to the team. You're sloppy! Unruly! Undisciplined! And you're soft! For this, you are going to do a morale run in full battle rattle. Twenty times around the compound. Now kit up and present yourselves on the parade ground. You got five minutes!"

"Yes, First Sergeant Ross!" they all shouted, none in disagreement with the order.

Logan turned to the barely awake Crncevic and said, "You too, Chief Crncevic. Since you chose not to take command."

After Logan returned empty handed and confronted Crncevic on his practical joke, Logan pressed him on whether he was actually going to take over command. Crncevic tried to get Logan to call him Milan, but the best Logan would acquiesce to was Chief. In the end, since Crncevic was not a seasoned battlefield warrior, he told Logan it was best for the safety of the team that he took command until they reached their destination. It was a decision Crncevic was now regretting.

"Moral of the story," David said to everyone after their frigid hip deep in snow run. "If you pull a practical joke on your First Sergeant, who runs a tight command, be prepared to suffer payback by getting run into the ground."

The trip to Iowa that under pre-war conditions could have been completed in under two days of non-stop travel, had now taken the team nearly four months. As the team exited out of the Iowa territorial capitol and headed east toward Iowa City to FOB Julien, the 31-year-old woman who had brought Logan into sexually active maturity was ever present in his mind. Des Moines was deserted, as Omaha had been. From what Logan's team had discovered in their travels, one detonated DNA bomb had a lethality range of up to 130-miles in radius. Omaha was roughly 114 miles from the territorial capitol using highway I-80 E. FOB Julien was almost the same distance from Des Moines using the same highway. The capitol would have certainly been a primary target. Providing Dubuque was not hit, the city was out of Des Moines' radius. However, Madison, WI, that territory's second largest populated city, put Dubuque in the extermination zone, being 94 miles away. Logan came to the realization that Dubuque would have suffered the same catastrophic collateral damage as had so many outlying populations had suffered—extinction. This was the reason Joyce Michaels and her daughter Sylvia were heavy on Logan's mind. It was distressing as well as disheartening to him. The team could have easily made a detour to Joyce's home. Except Logan didn't want to know. If he found them both dead, it would be heartbreaking for him. Not knowing was better. At least then there was a possibility that Joyce and Sylvia were still alive.

From the direction they were travelling on IA-27 S, the exit they needed to use to get to the base put them in sight of the base's rear perimeter wall. If someone was occupying the base and the wall guardhouse towers were being crewed, their approach would be detected far before getting to the exit ramp. Logan knew it put them at a tactical disadvantage if anyone had taken over the base. If it was occupied, then they would avoid it. They could certainly scavenge more diesel fuel and food along the way. It was just easier to use the fuel depot at the base. When the Iowa Territorial Guard Readiness Center had been re-designated as FOB Julien, it had also been given an expansion. The Territorial Army of the Republic had commandeered the Johnson County Road Department to its west, using part of it as a heliport and the rest as a billet area. Bordering the western wall was a heavy thicket of trees and then a large farmer's field. The walls of the base were not tall enough to see over the trees for the reason they had not been designed for outward observation, except to watch the buffer area between the trees and the wall.

There was a back route to that side of the base. They used an earlier exit, cut across a couple of pastures, and then onto a back road going south. Three-quarters of the way they headed east by cutting across three or four sections of fields and ended up on a less travelled road by a dense area of trees. It put them out of sight of the base but near to the intersecting road they needed to take for the base's entry.

Every Puma II vehicle, no matter the configuration, included a 4-rotor, short-range aerial scouting drone that could be used for day or night operations. The drone was capable of flying high for coverage of up to a quarter mile at 400 feet to get a bird's-eye view of large areas. It could also fly low to give more precise pictures with its 8k high-dynamic-range imaging resolution and multispectral/thermal imaging sensors that could pick up heat signatures.

Every Puma II crew squad member was trained on every system of the vehicle in case a crew member was killed or rendered incapaci-tated. Every drone on every Puma II was identical, and had a flight time of 70 minutes with a maximum operating distance of 2.54 miles. They were close enough to FOB Julien that their recon could be done with the drone inside the safety of the Puma.

When the drone approached, it was clear by the activities inside that the base was occupied. Further surveillance showed that many of the people were in uniform. Except, the uniforms worn were from The Republic as well as the UTA. It looked like the opposing sides had found a new home and were living in peaceful co-existence. That's what Logan and his team thought, and were ready to recall the drone and move on. As the drone made a pass over the area that had once been an outdoor caged internment camp for captured enemy combatants who were awaiting transfer, the team saw the jail was still occupied. Bringing the drone in for a closer look, they were shocked to discover a large number of prisoners huddled around two hobo barrels trying to stay warm. The two fires were not burning brightly, the captives were underdressed for the chill of the day, and the shelter cover to help protect its detainees from the elements was no longer in place. A majority of the caged were young females.

This now did not appear to be a harmonious place where everyone was working together to survive. It was the strong taking advantage of the weak. Logan was certain that something nefarious was happening. It did not sit well with any of them. The team formulated a tactical plan to liberate the hostages. It wasn't just their soldierly duty to help, it was a moral obligation to save the prisoners.

Content and lazy, and most likely over confident that no one would dare oppose them, the occupying group's security measures were "lax." There were two guards at the outdoor prison area, two together walking the main compound, one at the main gate, and only two in the guardhouses on the walls. One wall guard was at the main entry and another atop the rear wall. Heat signatures picked up another twenty-three inside the main building but there was no way to tell if any of them were civilians. What was needed was a covert infiltration late at night when most of the hostiles were asleep.

The plan was for David to stay back and operate the drone as over-watch, so the remainder of the team could adjust the mission as it went along. Logan and Marc would scale the western 12-foot wall at the guardhouse. Once situated inside the observation post, Logan, being a marksman—having honed his skill in his backyard shooting soda cans with various caliber rifles—would eliminate the wall sentries and the guards watching over the jail area using his sound suppressed, bolt-action Barrett Mk 24 Mod 2 MRAD ASR—multi-role adaptive design, advance sniper rifle. It was chambered in long range .338 Norma Magnum rounds with a 10 round detachable box magazine, and an effective range of 1,600 yards. Logan affectionately nicknamed it "Big

Mama." Afterward, Marc would slip over the wall and make his way to the main entry to take that guard out. Marc would then open the gate just enough to allow Benny and his team inside. Listening to David's communications, Logan would remain in his perch until the two roaming guards came into his sight, and then kill them. Once phase one was complete, Logan would make his way to the back of the compound and disable the solar inverters. After the lights were out, Benny, Marc, and Milan would use their night vision goggles to cross the compound to the entry of the main building. Logan would enter from the rear. Using the heat signatures of the occupants, David could guide the assault team through the building for optimal mission success.

The plan should have gone without incident but it didn't. In part it was Logan's fault. Once he came over the wall into the base, he should have gone straight to the inverters at the rear of the property. Instead, he went to check on the prisoners. A couple of the men became noisy, shouting to be set free when Logan approached. Logan told them to keep quiet if they wanted to live, but the two caged men kept protesting loudly, claiming that if Logan failed the prisoners would suffer greatly. The clamor got the attention of someone inside the building. A male voice began calling over the dead men's radios, asking what all the commotion was about. Logan had no choice but to pick up one of the dead guards' radios and respond. He told the person on the other end that two male prisoners were fighting over a female. The man on the other radio told Logan to kill both of them if they refused to stop, or there would be hell to pay. Lucky for Logan the enemy didn't realize Logan wasn't one of his own responding. Except, the loudest incarcerated antagonist refused to keep quiet. He started to shout to bring attention to Logan. Logan had no choice but to shoot the prisoner to silence him. The man instantly collapsed to the ground from the bullet that passed through his leg. Logan warned the others that if they didn't keep the injured man quiet, none of them would be let out. A group of women seized the bleeding man and held his mouth closed.

Logan was late getting to the inverters, but David radioed that everything was clear and he could proceed. In less than two minutes after the power was cut, two combatants came out the rear building entry. Logan was ready for them. They barely got four feet from the building's threshold when Logan put a bullet through each of their foreheads with his pistol.

Under the cover of darkness, and sound suppressed weapons, Logan and his team moved room to room with David's guidance, and quickly eradicated the enemy combatants. The team had located five non-combatants inside. Four of them were teenage girls. Then there was Lieutenant Kristen Leger, MD, legged chained but in unlocked room by herself.

Kristen Leger was born and raised in Brick Township, New Jersey. She had been educated at John Hopkins University, Baltimore as a surgeon, and then did her four-year residency at Johns Hopkins Hospital. Afterward, she got a trauma surgeon position at Northwestern Memorial Hospital, Chicago. A year later came the secession and formation of The Republic. War was the farthest thing on most people's minds. Sure, there had been troop movements on both sides to territorial borders to strengthen defenses. There was also a lot of posturing and threats from the Sovereign of the UTA regarding retaliation on those who seceded. But war? *No!* Most Americans believed the dispute between The Republic and the UTA would be peacefully resolved, as did Kristen. So, she remained in Illinois instead of returning to her childhood hometown in New Jersey. However, Sovereign Trumbull was determined to make the Territories of The Republic pay dearly for their seditious act. Nearly four months after The Republic seceded, Trumbull declared war on The Republic, and then had his troops begin with invading the Pennsylvania District of the Middle Colonial Territory. Pennsylvania first because the territorial governor and the district's superintendent had been the first two to sign the document of secession.

It didn't take long before the UTA pressed Doctor Leger into the service of their Medical Corps. There really hadn't been a choice for her. It was either join the Medical Corps, the non-combat specialty branch of the UT Army Medical Department, or be placed in an internment camp for being a suspected Republic collaborator. It had been a trumped-up accusation but under the UTA articles of war, there was no way to fight the charge since she had been deemed an enemy spy. Upon signing her enlistment papers, Kristen was given the officer rank of First Lieutenant and assigned as a battalion surgeon in a newly built installation outside of Decatur, Ill.

When the bombs came Decatur was not a target, Indiana was. Indiana was too far east for Decatur to be affected. The base lost communications with other UTA units. They did, however, pick up some civilian chatter on citizens band radio about the bombs not being nuclear but possibly a biological weapon based on the results of the detonations. After a few days a squad was sent out to investigate. A few hours later the base lost communication with them, and they never returned. Nine days later there was insurrection amongst the troops. The loyalists, mainly commissioned officers, wanted to remain and continue the fight, but the rest wanted to go home. They outnumbered the loyalists. The diehard officers lost. Those who survived the skirmish stripped the base of all its supplies and vehicles. Kristen had the misfortune of getting a ride with a small column that said they were heading east. They weren't. They were heading south. She had been kidnapped. A day after, they ran into a group of Republic soldiers heading north. There was a firefight. Her kidnappers were killed and she came out of it unscathed. Her misfortune, though, hadn't changed. The group that won were going to gang rape her, and most likely kill her afterward. Kristen made a bargain with them. Keep their "filthy cocks" out of her "chucky," which was Jersey girl slang for vagina, and she would patch up their wounded. The group first laughed at her offer and began slapping her around attempting to beat her into submission. She finally was able to scream out she was a surgeon, and she was wearing a uniform from the Medical Corps to prove it. The group wasn't totally convinced but accepted her deal anyway, providing the two injured survived. A couple of days later, Kristen crossed into Iowa and to FOB Julien.

The prisoners had been freed, fed, and Kristen had examined and medically tended to their individual needs. Logan and his team would get a few hours rest and re-fuel before leaving at 1:00 p.m. What little food remained at the base was not military issued, and Logan planned on giving it to the survivors. If anyone knew how to use a firearm, he would also give them one from the collection they had taken from the enemy dead.

By 7:00 a.m., freezing temperatures and a frigid wind swept in. An hour later it began to snow and a gale spun it around making visibility poor. A half-hour later, a heavy dumping snow storm arrived. For the beginning of the second week of April, the weather was unusual. The slow-moving storm they had gotten ahead of in Nebraska had caught up to them. Heavy blowing snow and frigid weather may have caused the team's travel plans to be pushed back, but there was work that could be done. The Quonset huts set up for the billet area needed to be checked over. Anything of use needed to be seized and inventoried. To be certain, Logan didn't want any survivor infighting of who should get what or who deserved more.

The Quonset huts had all been ransacked. There were no weapons or food to be found inside. There were, however, plenty of clean uniforms, overcoats, and boots the survivors could certainly use. Once a few of the huts were straightened up, Logan had the survivors assigned to them, separating the few men from the girls and women. Logan wasn't preventing anyone from leaving. If anyone wanted to leave, they were free to take the few vehicles there were and depart. Only the man who Logan shot wanted to take a chance in the storm, but then found that the bullet wound to his right leg prevented him from using the vehicle's gas pedal. The man cursed Logan for it, but Logan told him he was lucky he just didn't kill the man for jeopardizing everyone's lives. After the billet area, they made sure the latrine hut and the shower hut were up and running.

By late day there was a considerable amount of snow accumulation. Both of Logan's vehicles could navigate it without difficulty, but Logan knew it would be treacherous and slow going in the blinding snow. It was simpler and safer to stay put for a few days. Hopefully the weather would warm up quickly and melt away the freak snow storm accumulation.

Later in the evening 1LT Leger requested to speak to the ranking officer and not to the first sergeant again, not realizing that her initial conversation with Logan was with the squad's commander. It took her a moment to comprehend how small the team had been that took over.

"So, are you planning on keeping me in leg shackles?" Kristen asked in a perturbed tone.

Logan held up the keys and dangled them before her, but didn't make any attempt at releasing her. He was hoping she would ask politely. She didn't.

"If you think I'm going to get down on my knees for those keys."

"Is that assumption your window on the situation, Lieutenant? Let me wipe it clean so the light can shine through. You told me you were a prisoner here but yet you were held in an inside room that was unlocked. And compared to the rest of the prisoners that were held outside, you look pretty healthy and unabused." Logan threw her the keys before she could answer, and continued, "As I said earlier, I would need to verify your story. Every survivor vouched for you, with exception of the ass snapper I shot in the leg. Additionally, they're all very grateful for what you were allowed to do for them."

Kristen tossed the shackles aside and said, "It was barely anything. Unfortunately."

"Sometimes even doing a little can mean much to someone in need. So, what's your plan?"

"Plan? I'll tell you what my plan is," she said loudly with irritation. "To stay here and wait until the rest of those motherfuckers return so I can cut off their fucknuggets."

"Holy stink pickle, Lieutenant. Language, please!?" Logan commented in shock at her vocabulary choice.

"Bah Fongool," Kristen shot back.

"Why the hostility? I'm not the one who pissed in your boots."

"No, but you've half-assed everything," she said, and quickly added, "You think these half-a-dozen motherfuckers you killed were actually in charge? Fuck, no. All you have done is get rid of a few dipshit lackies and the second degenerate in charge. What happens to these women once you pull out in a day or two? I'll tell you. They'll be hunted down and find themselves right back here, or someplace else. This group of people are the scum of the military. Kidnappers, rapists, pedophiles, murders. You need to finish the job."

Logan understood Kristen's frustration if what she said was true, but he didn't like her ungrateful, hostile attitude. And he told her so.

"Well, I'm an idiot. I could have sworn the invite said 'rescue party'," Logan sarcastically returned. "Now why don't you put that attitude of yours in check, and give me a proper sitrep, so I can understand what has transpired here."

"I'm from Jersey. I was born with attitude," she told him.

Kristen realized she had vented her hostilities and anger at the wrong party. She gave Logan a full rundown of what she had seen and heard in her time at the base. The leader and the other half of his crew were due back tomorrow. It didn't leave much time for Logan to prepare.

Logan and his team weren't looking for another fight, but Kristen had been right with what she had explained. The group that had taken over the base was not only military scum but the scum of humanity. They were pillaging nearby inhabited communities, demanding that the survivors supply them with food and ammunition, things they had not found when they took over the abandoned base. Instead of just holding the females as hostages until the townsfolk handed over what they wanted, the group chose to kidnap them and trade them back days later. This was done solely for their own depraved sexual gratification.

Logan's plan for eliminating the second group wasn't sophisticated. It was simply to act as if everything was normal and let the group through the gate, and then ambush them. The group returned the day Kristen had said, just very late in the evening. It was lucky that Kristen had told him everything she knew about the group. It had helped in the deception, especially when the returning convoy had radioed they were going to be late. Logan made sure the radio conversation on his end was kept brief and made it appear that they were having transmission problems. It had been enough to fool them.

When the raiders radioed the base that they were a half hour out, the team took up their tactical stations. Logan positioned himself in one of the overhead watch towers of the main entry, while David took position inside the main gate's sentry hut. Benny and Marc took up position just inside the compound like they were on patrol. Also, so that their ruse would not be suspect, Logan had some of the captives return to their outside cage with Milan standing guard over them. Since the wind was still blowing and the snow falling, the team covered their faces and wore protective eyewear to mask their features. They hoped that the weather, the night, the facial coverings, and the appearance everything being normal would give the returning marauders no reason to be suspicious.

The plan was to get all three vehicles past the entry gate before attacking. It was also imperative they make sure the enemy had not returned with any more hostages before starting their assault. Logan gave a wave of acknowledgement as the enemy vehicles approached, and then signaled for David to open the gate. Both David and Logan kept a watchful eye on the group as they proceeded into the base. The first two vehicles were both Special Purpose All-Terrain Vehicles with turret mounted 12.7mm heavy machine guns. neither of which had gunners tending them. As the vehicles entered, Benny and Marc casually moved toward the lead truck. David radioed to his team that the first two trucks were clear of any civilians. The last truck was a 2.5-ton, 4x4 Medium Tactical Cargo truck, but it had its cargo bay frame canvas closed at the tailgate. David moved quickly to it to check it. There was no ladder or step up, so David had to grab on to the drop-down cargo door and put a foot onto the vehicle's hitch mount to get himself up. Someone inside grabbed an arm and hoisted him into the back or the truck. When David got inside, he told the person that had helped him, "Thanks," and then turned his rifle on the two occupants and shot them. The vehicle's driver must have either seen David go to the back of the vehicle or noticed the entry gate had not been shut after passing through. A few seconds after David eliminated the two cargo passengers, the truck stopped.

After killing the two hostile combatants, and then quickly radioing his team the cargo truck was clear, David heard two grenade blasts. The assault on the enemy convoy had begun. After pitching a grenade under each of the all-terrain vehicles' chassis, they began a weapons assault on them. Both vehicles attempted to get personnel into their weapons stations, but Benny and Marc swiftly took them out before either could return fire.

As David began to climb out of the cargo truck, the vehicle began to reverse. Logan saw him struggling to get out. There was nothing he could do but open fire at the vehicle's cab, hoping he could kill the driver. By the time David managed to get clear, the cargo truck had already backed out of the gate.

Logan had hoped to avoid destroying any cargo. He wanted to keep the supplies and return them to the people they were taken from, but it wasn't going to be possible. Logan had a contingency in place in case anything went sideways. Inside his perch, Logan had brought an AT6 rocket launcher with him. The AT6 was an 86mm unguided, portable, single-shot recoilless smoothbore light anti-armor weapon intended to give infantry units a means to destroy or disable armored vehicles and fortifications, but not tanks. Logan had made sure they packed a half dozen of them from the Ari-Cal-Nev Garrison, just in case. The AT6 annihilated the truck, and killed the driver and passenger.

Three days later warmer weather returned. Two days after that, Logan and crew helped those kidnapped get back to their families, which took them three days. After a day's rest, they refueled and headed east, taking the foul-mouthed Jersey girl with them. The team was now a coalition squad, and were happy to finally be heading toward the Middle Colonial Territory and home. First stop, Brick Township, New Jersey.

From Dubuque they went south to Davenport, IA and then southeast to Peoria, IL. Crossing the Upper Peoria Lake, they took UT-24 east. Along the way they passed through many small communities with survivors but made no stops, except to scavenge for fuel. They had been making good time toward the District of New Jersey with no setbacks, until they reached the PA-711 overpass on the I-70, Donegal, PA. There was a large commercial airliner that had crashed onto the highway. There was an immense debris field and the overpass had been demolished, blocking the way. From the wreckage the team determined the plane had been heading away from Pittsburgh. It wasn't a horrible setback. The PA Turnpike Donegal Interchange was a quarter-mile behind them. They could re-route and use PA-31, which would still take them to Somerset, PA.

The new route was very rural. As they drove out of Donegal Township, both sides of the roadway were lined with trees that were heavy with new Spring foliage. Just past a road sign that stated they were nearing the Laurel Hill Trout Farm, a large primate darted from one side of the roadway to the other and disappeared into the tree line. Logan and Kristen were sitting atop the vehicle in the commander's hatch, when the stocky animal ran by. Neither could believe what they just had seen. Logan ordered the vehicles to stop.

"Did you just see what I think we just saw?" Logan asked Kristen.

She exclaimed, "Oh, hell ya, I saw it!"

Logan radioed to his team again, "Heads on a swivel. Point vehicle just saw a… Some kind of large primate."

Benny and Milan were in the rear vehicle, they thought Logan was trying to make a joke. David confirmed the sighting, describing it as, "Fucking King Kong just ran by."

King Kong was an apt description for what they had witnessed, though Marc, who was sitting behind the video monitor station, couldn't confirm what the furry blur had been. Kristen said it appeared to have been a Western Lowland Gorilla, except the normal stature of that primate was only 4 to 5-½ feet when standing on two feet. The one they saw had to have been at least 10 feet tall and over 800 pounds.

Proceeding cautiously, the two vehicles slowly drove a half mile when David stopped the Puma right before the entry to the trout farm. Ahead, there was flesh, fur, and blood strewn all over the road. It looked like some type of animal had been ripped apart. Though concerning, the remains would not hamper their journey. David was standing in the driver's hatch next to Logan's position looking at the mutilated carcass, and its severed head, when gunfire began striking the Puma. David and Logan dropped back into the vehicle. Logan was securing his command hatch and didn't immediately see David had been hit. David had taken a round to his neck and was bleeding profusely. Logan cried out for Kristen, as he put pressure on the wound. There wasn't much room in the drive module, so Marc and Logan had to move him into the mission module, while Kristen kept pressure to David's wound. By the time they got him on the floor, David had lost a horrendous amount of blood from the bullet that had penetrated his carotid artery. The slug hadn't severed the artery completely, but it had been severely torn. Benny was radioing, trying to tell Logan that the vehicles had been surrounded by enemy forces and wanted orders. Marc checked the external surveillance cameras and saw nearly two dozen teenagers and youngsters pointing automatic rifles at them and an AT6 light anti-armor weapon at the Heavy Guns Carrier.

Kristen knew war-time penetrating carotid injuries were significantly lethal with a 22% mortality and morbidity rate. The presence of shock was associated with a higher mortality rate of 41%, compared with 8% with no-shock. David was in shock and had lost a significant amount of blood. The severity of David's penetrating trauma made surgical repair outside a trauma facility impossible, though it didn't stop her from trying to get David's bleeding under control.

As hard as Kristen tried, she couldn't save David. Logan was livid. He was going to make the sons-of-shit-biscuits pay for what they had done. He radioed Benny and told them to get ready to fire their machine gun, upon hearing the forthcoming explosion. He also told Marc the same. Logan grabbed a grenade and went to the commander's hatch. Opening it, he heard someone outside shouting for everyone to come out and surrender or they'd blow the back truck up.

Logan shouted he was coming out and for them not to shoot. He slowly appeared, showing himself to the outside. There was a group of dirtied, armed children and teenagers, both boys and girls. The ragtag bunch were not trained warfighters, but just a pack of punk-ass kids who had no compunction in killing.

"Put your hands up and get out of the truck, or we'll blow up your friends," a teenage boy demanded. The teen couldn't have been more than 15 years old.

Logan saw the AT6 but couldn't tell if it had already been expended. It didn't matter, he was determined to get payback.

"I take it you're the head prick of this group," Logan said.

"Fuck you," the leader returned. "We're taking your truck. Now you and the rest get out or we'll blow you to fucking hell. Put up your hands and get out. *Now!* Everyone. You got five seconds." The leader gestured to the kid who was holding the AT6, and told him. "On my order."

Logan feigned he was going to get out, "Okay. You win. Don't, don't shoot."

Logan put his left hand up on the lip of the hatch, and made like he was complying. As he rose his right hand came up. "Fuck you all to hell," he told the leader as he simultaneously tossed out the grenade. Logan dropped back down, just as the grenade hit the ground. Two seconds later it exploded.

Logan called through his radio headset, "Go loud, go loud," which meant for his team to crew the guns and start shooting.

Maybe there had been six seconds between the time Logan gave the order and Marc and Milan popped up into the turrets to fire, when a 12-foot gorilla came charging out of the woods and started grabbing up the injured kids and violently tossed them in various directions. Logan had no ill will or malice against the savage beast. He immediately ordered his team to stand down and move out. As the vehicles slowly pulled away, the gorilla turned toward them. Standing fully erect, the primate made very loud screaming sounds and at the same time very rapidly beat its chest with its left hand. When the vehicles had moved far enough away that the gorilla no longer perceived Logan and his team as a threat, the gorilla took the teenage boy it was clutching around the ankles with its right hand, and began to thrash the youth like a stick on the ground, bashing the kid's skull until it cracked open and his brain matter oozed out. The gorilla threw the group's leader aside, and then fled.

Distraught, Logan climbed back onto the top of the Puma so that no one could hear his sorrow. His tears were so abundant that he had to remove his tactical shooting glasses and CCFC to wipe his face. Never before had Logan shed tears over the loss of those under him. That wasn't to say he didn't want to mourn every loss, like he had when Carol King had been killed. He just couldn't. He had to remain strong and not show weakness to his superiors or subordinates. But the death of David had cut him to his core. He, like Benny and Marc, had gone to school together and had enlisted together. They were all friends and there was now one less of them because of a senseless act of violence perpetrated by a bunch of ruthless and heartless kids with guns. Was this what was left of humanity: rapists and killers? Is that what he would find when he got back to their hometown? If that was the case, he felt that those who had launched the DNA rockets into America had done the world a disservice by not wiping out all the country's inhabitants. He took his face mask and threw it to the wind in disgust of the thought, and the realization that with the decimation of the populace maybe the virus had been wiped out too. He just didn't care at the moment.

Whether by luck or divine intervention, Logan looked up from staring at his blood-stained hands and saw a sign to the Bakersville Cemetery. Logan truly wanted to take David's body back home for burial but he knew it impractical. They had no body bags and they were going to New Jersey first.

The cemetery was on a hill off a side road. It was an old cemetery, made up of many memorial markers going as far back as 1846. Logan, Marc, and Benny decided together where they should bury their friend.

It was a good spot, under a large oak tree near to the edge of the woods opposite the road. They did the best they could with the marker, lashing some wood together with rope, and then with a knife carving out his rank, name, and dates upon it. Standing in front of David's grave, Logan ordered, "Attention!" The team raised a saluting hand and remained in posture as Logan continued, "Our flag does not fly because the wind moves it. It flies with the last breath of each soldier who died protecting it. Sergeant David George, we thank you for your service."

The entire team repeated, "Thank you for your service."

Logan declared, "Carry on," and then executed the salute.

They made camp there that night, and decided not to leave until late the next morning. They wanted and needed to have some time to celebrate the memory of their friend and fellow soldier. Discarding their face coverings, they sat around a well-lit campfire. Logan had brought out an unopened bottle of Lagavulin Distillers Edition Double Matured Single Malt Islay Scotch Whisky for their second round of consumption. The bottle had been David's. He had scavenged it from out of the rare liquor display case from a store in Phoenix, as they had done with the other alcohol they had been drinking along the way. David had said he had never had it, but since it was dated 2034, it must taste amazing. However, no matter how hard Logan tried to get David to open it to share, David refused. He said it was only going to be opened once they got back home.

On the third pass of the bottle, and Logan's second toast to David, Logan loudly exclaimed, "Fuck! That monkey had some serious anger issues."

"I'd be angry, too, if I had a dick as small as his," Marc remarked.

Logan added, "Guess whatever caused him to so enormous also shrunk his trunk."

"You'd never know it by looking at them, but male gorillas have surprisingly tiny penises," Kristen informed them. "About 1.5 inches when erect."

"That doesn't seem fair," Benny commented.

"That's because in gorilla society, male silverbacks fuck a lot of females who are all monogamous to him. No reproductive competition equals tiny dick," Kristen enlightened them. "Speaking of dicks, which one of you virgins wants to get lucky tonight?" she announced, but was looking directly at Benny.

Benny hadn't noticed Kristen was eying him until he saw the others looking at him.

"Why is everyone looking at me?" Benny asked, and then turned to Kristen, who was seated next to him. "Oh, no. I'm definitely not the only virgin—*Male!* Male here." The crew began to laugh at Benny's accidental admission. Benny tried to deflect the unwanted attention. "What about Marc?"

"Yeah, nice comeback," Logan mocked.

"I'm not the one she's looking at, Benny," Marc assured him. "And you know I have a girl back home."

"Well, Sergeant Lee? Care to play doctor? I gotta few things we can probe each other with," Kristen imparted with a smirk.

"See, that kinda shit scares me. Besides, you're a team member. That would be like having sex with my sister."

"You don't have a sister," Logan reminded him.

"Yeah, but if I did," Benny clarified.

"It'd be much better, I'd be awake," Kristen told him with certainty.

"Ouch!" Milan exclaimed.

"Not funny," Benny told everyone as they laughed.

Kristen thought she'd try one more time using titillation instead of her domineering Jersey girl insistence to get what she desired. After all, she really was attracted to Benny. He was strong, handsome, and respectful. He kept calling her ma'am, even though her officer rank didn't matter anymore. Even his boyish naivete was a turn on to her. She really wanted to be with him. Also, the liquor and him sitting close to her had made her really horny. Benny on the other hand thought Kristen excessively brash, bold, and foul-mouthed. This was perfectly fine for him in the context as fellow soldiers. It wasn't like he or Logan didn't curse it up every once in a while. He did find Kristen physically attractive with her blonde-hair, sparkling hazel eyes, and her shapely figure that nicely filled out her uniform. Except, Benny always imagined his first sexual dalliance would be of his initiative in a romantic setting, not in a cemetery with a sexual partner who was aggressively looking for some quick gratification.

Kristen leaned over to him, and with due sincerity whispered in his ear, "If you don't have sex with me tonight, I'll have to have solo sex, which won't be a tenth as good as we can accomplish together."

Under the campfire's ample glow, the group saw Benny's expression. Benny blushed at the revelation. Though her admission was overly candid, her words were almost sweet, Benny thought. If she had said this to him privately the first time, he would have given it some consideration. She had not. Kristen had put him on the spot and had embarrassed him in front of the team. And the cemetery thing kind of creeped him out, anyway.

"Still no," he told her.

Kristen didn't say another word. She got up, went over to Milan, grabbed the Lagavulin from him, and disappeared into the tree line.

Logan knew why Kristen had disappeared and why she wanted to fuck Benny. It had nothing to do with sex, Logan was certain of this. Logan shook his head with disappointment, and said, "Benny, Benny, Benny. What I'm about say, I say with all due respect and love as your friend. You're an idiot."

"Wait. *What?* I'm an idiot? How does her being rude, crude, and wanting to fuck me in a grave yard make me an idiot?" Benny demanded clarification.

"It isn't just about sex," Logan began. "It's about her need for physical intimacy and companionship for the night. She's lonely and wanted the sweetest guy on the team for comfort."

"That's crazy. And sweet!? I'm not sweet," he denounced Logan's comment.

"Oh, really?" Marc said and rebutted with, " 'Yes, ma'am.' 'Right away, Lieutenant.' 'Can I help you with that, ma'am?' That's sweet."

It was true and Benny knew it. He didn't have to address her as ma'am or Lieutenant Leger; he chose to, and he didn't know why. Maybe, it was because she scared the crap out of him and was afraid to

call her Kristen. Instead of admitting to it, he scoffed at Marc's observation and made an excuse for it. "That's cause she's older and out
ranks me."

"That's really lame, Benny," Logan remarked.

"Did you see the way she limped out of here? Milan asked.
"Clearly, she was hurt by the rejection."

Logan added, "Yeah, and tomorrow, she'll act like nothing's wrong,
like it never happened. And she'll never ask you again. And that will
be a tragedy."

Benny called Logan out on his supposed wisdom of women. "Since
when did you become an expert on women?"

"I'm not," Logan admitted. "However, I base my observation and
insight on experience. Remember the woman in Dubuque I spent a few
hours with? As scary and as traumatic the experience was losing my
virginity to a woman who was around Kristen's age, I realized later it
had nothing to do with sex." Logan reached into a pocket on his
tactical vest and pulled out a small box. Opening it he told everyone,
"Joyce gave me this ring. She said she wanted me to have it, so I could
give it to that special woman she knew was out there for me. I didn't
want to take it, but she insisted. She said that I had given her something that she hadn't had in a very long time. I asked her what she
meant but all she would say was that I would understand some day.
Well, I figured it out the day we thought we were going to be blown
into radioactive hell. Joyce was as sacred, lonely and in need of
comfort that night as much as I was waiting for the nukes to drop. And
I wished at that moment I could have felt the physical intimacy and
emotional comfort that Joyce must had felt during our brief interlude
together." Logan took a breath and then closed the ring box. "Kristen's
tough-ass, foul-mouth Jersey girl attitude is mostly for show. She's
afraid to be perceived as weak and vulnerable. But deep down, she's as
scared and lonely as the rest of us. So, as your friend, I'm imploring
you, go get another bottle and go find her. And don't worry about the
sex part. Because not even Kristen would truly be that desperate to
fuck you," he told Benny in deadpan, but then grinned widely after he
said it.

The team began to laugh.

Benny returned, "Oh, fuck you. And you, too, Marc. And let's not forget you, Chief," Benny said as he flipped them all off.

Still laughing, Logan told him, "Go on get out of here. Love ya, brother."

"Yeah, love you, too, asshole," Benny said as his parting shot before disappearing into the darkness.

"Alright, who's getting the next bottle?" Milan asked.

Bad weather seemed to dog them. By the time they rose in the morning, the temperature had fallen to the mid-40s, and dark clouds were rolling in. Before the team reached the Carlisle Barracks, where they planned to refuel, the weather turned decisively worse. It wasn't snow this time but a heavy downpour of rain accompanied by a high sustained wind. It became such a torrential downpour that visibility was near zero. Logan ordered the two vehicles to pull off the road and wait until the rain subsided enough that they could safely travel again. Luckily the convoy had been near to the PA Turnpike Cumberland Valley Service Plaza. Pulling into the plaza, they found the building had been boarded up. Upon further investigation they discovered that the fuel pumps had been padlocked.

It didn't take much for Milan to pry the plywood away from the main entry and gain access to the building. A quick recon of the structure's interior showed that the service plaza had been quickly abandoned. The convenience store and fast food chain stores inside appeared to be mostly stocked, though there was evidence of pilfering by rodents. In the dining areas there was a substantial amount of food wrappers and cups on tables. They talked amongst themselves to what had caused the service plaza to be boarded up and abandoned so quickly. Nearly two hours later the rain subsided. Logan decided it would be to their advantage to fuel up at the service plaza instead of finding a fueling depot inside the Carlisle Barracks. Locating the manholes for the underground fuel storage tanks wasn't difficult and neither was siphoning enough diesel fuel. Within three hours of being sidelined by the rain, the convoy was again underway.

Continuing along the turnpike, it didn't take the team very long to figure out why the service plaza had been secured. As they drove closer to Mechanicsburg, the roadway ahead of them was littered with war machines from both sides. Some fighting vehicles were completely destroyed, while others were completely intact. Logan, Benny, and Marc had heard the UTA had made a second attempt to capture southern Pennsylvania, well after the three of them had fought in the first Pennsylvania border campaign. Except, that had been two years into the war. They had not heard the UTA had penetrated so deeply beyond the Maryland/Pennsylvania border. They reckoned this battle may have been happening just prior to the bombs falling, making it the third engagement in southern Pennsylvania. Mechanicsburg was seventy-five miles west of Philadelphia. This would certainly account for the lack of rotting corpses and why so many intact vehicles had been deserted.

The three of them remembered very well their first battle. Benny had saved Logan's life that first day. The three of them, along with David George, had managed to survive while so many others around them perished. The invasion had been a folly on the part of the UTA. The enemy had underestimated The Republic's resources as well as its resolve to remain self-governing.

Sovereign Trumbull thought it would be a symbolic start to the invasion of Pennsylvania by capturing Chambersburg, PA first, as the Confederate Army had done during their Gettysburg campaign during the first civil war. He believed if he could quickly capture Somerset, Chambersburg, Gettysburg, York, Lancaster, and Oxford, PA, UTA forces could then quickly swing east and capture Philadelphia. A decisive victory at Philadelphia would be a demoralizing defeat to the Territorial Republic of America and would put an end to the insurrection and force The Republic to rejoin the UTA.

Although Chambersburg had significance during the first civil war for the Confederate march to Gettysburg, it held no importance in modern times. However, Trumbull insisted, and being the sovereign and supreme commander of the military, he got what he demanded. Nevertheless, Sovereign Trumbull was no war strategist like main Confederate States Army General J.E.B. Stuart had been. Trumbull's ego got in his way, and he refused to listen to the advice of his military commanders. The invasion of Pennsylvania quickly turned to disaster for the UTA. They attempted to re-order their army and put down a firm defensive line against The Republic's counterattacks, but it was to no avail. The battles at Somerset and Chambersburg were scenes of utter carnage. The loss of life and equipment were devastating for both forces. In the end, The Republic's resolve was more than the UTA predicted, and they were forced to make a hasty retreat only after two days of engagement. The decisive victories for The Republic solidified their position of secession and proved to the UTA that they were committed in keeping their independence.

The convoy was midway through the battlefield when they saw a wet, uniformed man standing in the middle of the road with a shotgun held above his head. His uniform was not that of a Republic soldier but of a UTA sailor. The team was cautious in their approach. For all they knew there could still be active enemy forces about and they were driving into a trap.

The convoy stopped within 25 feet of the sailor. Logan popped out of the commander's hatch of the Puma with his weapon at the ready. The warfighter looked dog tired and pale.

"I surrender," were the only words the seaman got to say before he collapsed unconscious.

Dehydrated and malnourished was Kristen's diagnosis. Two bags of intravenous solution helped to rehydrate the late-30s man and bring him back to consciousness. After introductions and assurances that the sailor was not a prisoner of war, Logan asked how he came to be so far inland and in Republic territory. The mariner had a harrowing tale to tell.

Petty Officer 1st Class Peter Henley was an enlisted sailor aboard the Dreadnought 2050 class naval destroyer the UTS *Kara S. Hultgreen*, stationed out of Norfolk Naval Station, VA. The destroyer had been part of the UTA's naval flotilla that was tasked with patrolling the territorial waters of the Eastern Seaboard's North Atlantic region that extended from Maine to the Delaware/Maryland border. The fleet's purpose was to stop all supply ships from Europe that were bound for The Republic, and if necessary, to engage and destroy any combatant vessel that challenged them. They were mainly concerned about enemy submarines.

Peter's taskforce did not get a clear message as to who had launched the missiles on America. Neither of the two destroyers in the patrol fleet were able to intercept and destroy any incoming missile. He imparted that everyone was on edge after the attack, especially when neither the *Hultgreen* or their other three vessels were able to reach Norfolk Naval Station or any other UTA military installation. All communications had been lost. At first, they thought it was due to the EMP discharge by the nuclear detonations. Their onboard Joster EMP Detection System that had the ability to detect the source of an electro-magnetic pulse attack, including an attack's strength, frequency and direction, showed there had been no blast of electromagnetic energy. A couple of days later the ship's communication center began to pick up amateur radio broadcasts that major cities had been bombed with some sort of weapon that could disintegrate flesh, and that the toxin was being carried 80, possibly 100 miles outside the detonation zones.

A day later, the UTS *Christopher W. Grady,* another destroyer, radioed and stated that their Combat Information Center had sonar contact with a Republic submarine. The enemy vessel's established track had put it three miles out and on an intercept course with the *Grady.* They were going to hunt it down and destroy it. After the radio message, the UTS *Christopher W. Grady* was not heard from again.

The war, at least at sea, had not ended with the missile strike. The remaining ships continued their patrols and was actively seeking the submarine they believed had sunk the *Grady.* A week later, communication with combat ship UTS *Michael X. Garrett* was lost.

After months at sea, the remaining two ships were running low on food. With no resupply ship to service them, the UTS *Kara S. Hultgreen* had no choice but to return to its home port. This brought about dissention amongst a majority of the crew. They feared the biological or chemical agents used may still be lingering and would kill them, or perhaps it dissipated but the food supplies back at Norfolk Naval Station were now contaminated.

The UTS *South Carolina* was supposed to rendezvous with the *Hultgreen*, so they could head to port together. The *South Carolina* never made the rendezvous, and the *Hultgreen* was unable to raise them. A search of their last know position proved fruitful. There had been 18 survivors, who all stated it wasn't one submarine, but two that had attacked the UTS *South Carolina*. After the rescue, Henley's ship headed to port.

The UTS *Kara S. Hultgreen* did not immediately dock but remained a mile off shore. They first sent in two recon teams to check out the naval station, and to see if there were any hostiles on the base. There wasn't a lot of places that Norfolk Naval Station personnel could take refuge in against a nuclear attack. The days of fallout shelters were a thing of the far past. The main defense posture of the naval base was geared toward repelling more conventional attacks, such as missiles fired from enemy submarines or ships, and/or an air attack by planes or drones. That kind of attack was highly unlikely, though, because Norfolk was located in an area that would make any "Pearl Harbor' style attack an impossible task. Consider the fact that Virginia had 21 other active military installations, eight of which were Army posts. Both Langley Air Force Base and Naval Air Station Oceana, which are in nearby proximity, could have close air support aircraft in Norfolk's airspace within ten minutes. Fort Monroe, an Army installation that exists right across the river from the Norfolk Naval Base, would also supply support to Norfolk. As for a nuclear attack, the base relied on space tracking and surveillance satellites that reported data to information centers, and then onto military bases. Under ordinary conditions an attack could be thwarted. The civil war had broken down the reliability of those systems. They failed. The bombs fell. America was annihilated.

The teams checked the lower levels of many of the buildings, only to discover discarded uniforms and some strange residue. The sailors were horror struck when they realized what it meant. Even though the ship's commander had told the teams not to discuss their findings, word spread quickly through the ship. Eighty percent of the crew mutinied. Peter didn't want to commit mutiny but if it was the only way to get off the ship, then he was for it. Within an hour the mutineers had control of the destroyer. No one was critically injured or killed in the rebellion, though there were some injuries on both sides.

Henley left the UTS *Kara S. Hultgreen* with a half day's worth of food and three days of water from the ship. It was easily enough supplies to get him to his destination. Peter didn't want to take a chance of eating or drinking any food or water that was within 100 miles of a blast zone. Finding transport on the base, he headed toward the New York District. Not too far out of Chambersburg, shortly after sunset, Henley almost ran into a rangale of deer that were crossing the highway. He swerved his Joint Light Tactical Vehicle to avoid them, but subsequently crashed through the guardrail and rolled it over.

"Why come North?" Logan asked. "Didn't you want to go home?"

"My wife and son lived on base. I found them, or what was left of them. So, I headed out."

Logan asked again, "But why head into Republic territory?"

"Buffalo, New York. That's where I was headed... Some of the civilian radio transmissions we picked up said Buffalo hadn't been bombed. The Republic was taking in refugees. No matter who you fought for. The broadcast sounded official, and was being transmitted on three different channels"

"Why spare Buffalo?" Marc asked, rhetorically.

Milan answered, "Its proximity to Canada, I surmise. Must be the Canadians didn't want any residual contamination to cross over the Niagara River."

"Makes sense," Kristen said. "Wouldn't be surprised if other cities along the Canadian border were spared."

Logan told Henley he could get him closer to Buffalo, without walking, if he didn't mind taking a detour to New Jersey. This would also give the petty officer time to recuperate. PO1 Henley was glad for the lift. Along the way, Logan told him about his team and how Dr.

Kristen Leger had joined them, and where their destination was after Brick Township.

Brick Township, District of New Jersey, Middle Colonial Territory was like every city that was near a city that had been attacked: quiet, devoid of human life, and had the tell-tale signs that the inhabitants who once lived there had made a desperate attempt to flee. Kristen went home to an empty house. Logan didn't leave after taking her home. He waited patiently to give her privacy to grieve before he sent Benny to fetch her. Benny didn't hesitate. Logan had no idea what had happened between them the night before, and he didn't ask. All he knew was that neither had returned to camp until the sun came up.

She was in her bedroom sobbing. Benny put a hand on her shoulder for comfort. Kristen rose and grabbed onto him and pulled him close for comfort. They stayed locked together for nearly five minutes before Kristen calmed down. Benny told her to grab whatever she needed and to join the team on the rest of their journey. Perhaps his home was still there and she could make it hers, too. If not, then they all could find a place to make a new home. Either way, everyone wanted her to remain part of the team. Kristen didn't say a word. She gave Benny a quick kiss on the lips and then gathered up some personal items. There was no reason for her to remain in Brick Township, and many reasons to continue the journey.

PART III

HOME FIRES

It was late when they left Brick Township, and most everyone was a bit haggard from the previous night's drinking. They were just a few miles shy of Southfields, NY, when Logan decided it was best to get off Route 17 and find a place to bed down for the night. They exited off for Sterling Forest. Arriving at the four-way intersection at the top of the off ramp, Logan was peering out the commander's hatch trying to decide which way to go. His intuition told him right onto Kanawauke Road. Proceeding slowly, Logan was just looking for a spot to put them out of sight. They had just crossed over the Route 17 overpass, when Logan saw a small sign pointing left that read, "Ramapo River Access."

As they followed the dilapidated road to the water's edge, they found that they weren't the only ones who thought it was a good idea to get off the main road. In front of them was an 18-wheeler. Investigating they found the semi-truck door unlocked but no one inside. The semi-trailer still had the locks on the back and side doors. It wasn't until they scouted the area that they discovered a pile of discarded clothing. Logan's theory was that the trucker must have pulled off the road and stepped to the river's edge to enjoy mother nature one last time before the nukes fell. Unfortunately, Southfields was slightly over 50 miles from New York City. The trucker must have known he wasn't going to outrun the blast. The team was excited about the prospect of investigating the truck's contents, especially Logan, since the semi-trailer was from the store Two Guys.

Two Guys was America's oldest and number one discount store chain founded by brothers Sidney and Herbert Hubschman. When the brothers first started in 1946, they operated a snack bar concession in the Radio Corporation of America (RCA) plant in Harrison, New Jersey. It was at that time they created the Teardrop chocolate candy. The recipe remained almost unchanged ever since its creation. The team waited until morning light to investigate the truck's contents.

As Logan swung the rear doors open, he announced, "Two Guys, the Super Supermarket." It was the department store's catchphrase.

They were a bit disappointed to find the truck only had half a load of cargo. Opening the side trailer door to let in more light, Logan and

Benny checked through the pallets, while Marc and Milan were seeing if the truck was operational. Henley stood watch, shotgun in hand.

In the far back Logan found two crates of lever action .30-30 caliber hunting rifles and a couple of cases of ammunition. The lever-gun rifles weren't practical for defense; they could only hold five cartridges and barely had a 200-yard accuracy. It was a solid close-range hunting rifle though, and had ample power for shooting aluminum cans for target practice. Logan didn't bother with them. He had a few at home and they couldn't compare to either his military issued sniper or individual rifle.

They did discover a variety of canned foods. About six pallets worth of tomato sauce, solid white albacore tuna, chunk light tuna, baked pork and beans, whole kernel corn, spaghetti & meatballs, beef ravioli in tomato & meat sauce, cut green beans, cream of chicken soup, cream of mushroom soup, tomato soup, and chicken noodle soup. Logan wasn't surprised that the truck wasn't packed full of different foods. Even before the war the pandemic had slowed food manufacturing and shipments. The cut green beans and cream of mushroom soup were gladly received, two of Logan's favorites. As Benny and Logan began disassembling the clear wrapped pallets to pull out an assortment of cases for their food re-supply, Logan came across a single pallet of candy in the center of the canned food pallets. He started vigorously tearing it apart and removing the boxes. He was looking for the holy grail of confectionary delights—his beloved Teardrops, which he hadn't had since he joined the military. Logan kept tossing boxes of Beemans Chewing Gum, Necco Wafers, Mike and Ike Original Fruits, and Atomic Fireballs aside. Then toward the bottom came the chocolates: Hollywood Milk Shake bars, Hollywood Butter Nut bars, Chocolate Christmas Balls, Wrapped Purple White Chocolate Hearts. He thought maybe the war had put an end to its production. Finally, the last two boxes on the bottom of the pallet were Wrapped Light-blue Milk Chocolate Teardrops. Logan burst with excitement. "Yes!!! *Score.*" He showed Benny the box.

"Of course," Benny replied, knowing Logan's devotion and love of the confectionary.

Kristen came around to the end of the trailer and asked, "What's all the screaming about?"

Benny thumb gestured to Logan, as Logan walked to the end of the trailer. He set the two boxes of chocolates down at the open tailgate in front of Kristen.

"Chocolate?" Kristen questioned. "The way you were carrying on, I thought you were having an orgasm."

"I did," Logan said, and with affection quoted her the chocolate's catchphrase. "Teardrops. The chocolate that will bring you to joyous tears."

"Nah. Give me Hot Tamales cinnamon candy. That'll get the juices flowin'."

"Sorry. Only Atomic Balls."

"Bah," she scoffed with her Jersey girl attitude, dismissing Logan with a wave. "There's no substitute for the real thing," she told him.

Kristen was right. The Chocolate Christmas Balls and Milk Chocolate Stars he had found couldn't compare to a Teardrop. He loaded the two boxes of chocolate into the Puma. The food went into the two-wheel trailer. He wasn't selfish though; he did distribute a bag of chocolates to each of them.

With Marc's assistance Milan was able to get the semi-truck started. It only had a dead battery and wasn't difficult to jump start it using the HGC. Milan said he could drive it, if they wanted to take it with them. In the end though, Logan thought it best to just stay with their military vehicles, since it would take someone away from crewing the HGC's machine gun station if necessary. At least they had a stash of food they could come back to, if no one else came across it.

A little over two hours later, they rolled into the rural area of Delhi. They didn't go through the town, they came up a back route and went to Logan's home first. He lived outside of the main town along the Little Delaware River.

As the vehicles came through the long drive toward the house, a couple of horses were grazing in the front yard, which was peculiar, as was the lack of the yard being mowed. Logan's dad liked to keep the yard trim, even in April if the grass was long. Plus, his father would have never allowed the horses to trample the front yard. There were also chickens in the yard, which was even more strange since they never owned chickens.

Logan checked the house thoroughly, but his parents were nowhere to be found. Neither was his Dalmatian. The family SUV was gone, but his father's personal pickup truck and horse trailer remained. It wouldn't have been unusual for both his parents and his dog to not be home, except for the fact that Logan's home looked like it hadn't been inhabited in months. Logan headed out back toward the barn to see why the horses were roaming free, when he came across two makeshift burial plots. The markers had the names of his parents on them. It couldn't be, Logan thought to himself. He ran past Benny as Benny approached the back of the house. Benny saw the two markers, and then ran in the direction Logan had fled. The team told Benny that Logan bolted up the drive toward the street. Benny quickly followed on foot.

As Logan ran up the driveway to the Miranda's house, he discovered it burnt to the ground. He was standing staring at the remains when Benny caught up to him. Logan turned to his best friend and with despair asked, "What the hell happened here? What, Benny, what?" Then panicked, Logan told him, "Marc's house. Your house. We gotta go!"

Marc lived on the outskirts of town on a street called Park Place. It was another street the team didn't have to go through town to get to. Marc also found his home abandoned. This put him in a bit of a panic. He wanted to go check on his girlfriend Lisa Lawler. The team split up. Marc, Logan, and Henley took the Puma, and headed to the Lawler residence, while Benny, Milan, and Kristen went to the Lee home. They would radio one another when they had news.

The news was bad. There was no one home at either Benny's or Lisa's residence. It appeared the homes had been unoccupied for some time. As both teams had made their way to their respective destinations, they had made a horrible discovery. Delhi had been laid to ruins.

The two teams re-connected at Ross & Reynolds. Logan was relieved to find his father's establishment was still standing, and hadn't been ransacked or pilfered. Though, if you were looking for survival supplies in the form of food and beverage, you wouldn't find any with the exception of the soda machine out in front of the building. Ross & Reynolds didn't sell guns but they did carry ammo for bird, small game, and deer hunting but not in large quantities.

Logan was true to his word. Henley was closer to his destination. In further lending aid and assistance, Logan gave the petty officer the company pickup truck along with some food, water, a compressed hydrogen fuel canister, and two boxes 12-gauge cartridges for Henley's Mossberg tactical pump shotgun. If luck was with the sailor, hopefully he would be in Buffalo in under five hours.

With few exceptions, every business and residence along a two-mile strip of Main Street had been burnt to the ground. That was only the beginning of the devastation Logan and his team discovered. Over the next four hours they scoured the town's city limits looking for someone still living there. They discovered it hadn't only been the business district that had been destroyed.

Benny's father was a Professor of History and East Asian Studies at The District University of New York at Delhi (DUNY Delhi). Mr. Lee was a renowned scholar and had published three bestselling historical books: *The Rise and Fall of Communist China*, *The Korean Re-unification*, and *The History of The Greater Tibet Republic*. When they discovered that some of DUNY Delhi had partially been razed by fire, too, Benny began to tear up. With not finding his parents and part of the university destroyed, Benny felt lost and feared that his parents, like Logan's, were dead.

The university was just one of the many structures that had been levelled. The post office, the police station, the fire department, the Delaware County Sheriff's Office, the Delaware County Motor Vehicle Department, and a couple of churches that all were off the main business district to the west were also burnt to the ground. The only buildings of significance that hadn't been annihilated or even pillaged were the Delaware Academy Middle/High School and the health care center; all of which were on the eastern side of the West Branch Delaware River.

It appeared that Delhi had suffered a scorched-earth policy by invading UTA forces. Logan, Benny, and Marc were well aware of this punishment policy. It had happened when the UTA invaded the District of Pennsylvania. On the orders of the Sovereign, Pennsylvania was to be made an example of for their sedition because they had signed The Republic's declaration of secession first. Luckily, Pennsylvania had not felt the Sovereign's full intended wrath because the UTA had been pushed back across the border and back into the Southern Colonial Territory's Districts of Maryland and Virginia. However, Delhi was far away from Pennsylvania and from The Republic capital of Buffalo, NY. Could it have been the UTA had invaded the district capital of New York in Albany? Had UTA forces come southwest 90 miles to punish Delhi? But why? Logan thought to himself. The only thing significant Delhi had was the district university. It paled in comparison to the University at Albany. None of the scorched-earth policy made any sense.

In front of the main building entry to Delaware Academy the team discussed their options. Logan told everyone that they could stay with him if they wanted. The house had hydrogen and solar. They also could go back to Southfields and get the 18-wheeler. Benny wanted to continue looking for his parents. Marc wanted to find his parents as well as his girlfriend. Milan and Kristen were on board for whatever they decided. As Logan thought more about it, he decided he wanted to find someone who could tell him what had happened to his mother and father, and also, what had happened to Jessica and her parents. Marc, Benny, and Logan agreed they should check out some neighboring towns to see if they suffered the same plight. Hopefully, someone somewhere might know what happened in Delhi.

Bloomville was ten minutes to the northeast and the closest community when it came to significant population. However, if they went south along Route 10 to Walton, they would pass through four smaller communities. In Walton there was the Territorial Guard base, the place where Logan, Benny, Marc, and David had enlisted. If there was any place nearby that might still be populated, the three of them agreed it would be Walton.

Logan decided he wanted to drive the Heavy Guns Carrier, and use it as the lead vehicle with Milan in the gunner position. He had Benny take over the Puma driving to give Marc a break and re-assigned him to the turret gun. All of it was done to break up the boredom of their recent trip home, and it also gave different sets of eyes on the surroundings.

Instead of heading back to Main Street and then south, Logan took a side street that would intersect with Main. They were halfway down the side road when Logan had to make an abrupt stop. An indigent looking man darted out in front of the truck and stopped. Logan came within five feet of striking him. The scruffy looking man was dressed in clean clothes, but he was barefoot. Logan didn't immediately recognize the man, but then Logan understood he knew him. It was Jim H. Reynolds III, whose nickname was Scruffy because of his beard. The story behind the beard was that Jim had a baby face and he had gotten tired of people mistaking him for a teenager. So, he grew a beard to appear older. Logan didn't call him Scruffy. Jim Reynolds was the Ross & Reynolds' floor manager, and son of his father's business partner. Logan had worked part time for two summers under Reynolds before Logan enlisted. Though the two were well acquainted, they were not friends, and Logan thought it would be unprofessional to call his superior and co-owner's son by a nickname, though Reynolds did tell Logan it was okay to call him Jim.

Logan radioed to Marc and Benny that he was getting out of the truck and the two should join him.

"Jim!" Logan called out as he exited the truck. Reynolds didn't respond. As Logan drew closer, he called to Jim again. "Jim. It's me, Logan Ross."

Jim looked confused. He replied, "Im. Im Enols. Enols. Enols. Im Enols."

It was clear to Logan that something had happened to Jim. Before he could ask what was wrong, an older man came running toward them, begging not to hurt Jim.

"Please, I beg of you. Don't hurt him, he's harmless," the man pleaded.

Astonished, Logan questioned, "Principal Weiss?"

The woman looked at Logan, and then to Marc and Benny, but didn't acknowledge she knew the group.

"Principal Weiss. It's Logan Ross." Logan pointed, "And Benny Lee, and Marc Romano. Do you remember us?"

Logan Ross?" Emma Weiss questioned. "You're the boy whose father owned the feed store with Jim's father. Yes, I remember. I remember you, too, Benny. You two got in trouble in the school cafeteria with Gino Madanello and that Miranda girl from the middle school. I gave you all detention."

Jim became irritated and began pounding a fist to his head, and repeating, "Go mando. Hurt, hurt, bang, bang."

"What happened to Jim, Ms. Weiss?" Logan asked with concern.

"Don't rightly know. Think it might have been the Scavs when they came back and set the university on fire. Someone found Jim on Bronco Drive, lying in his own blood with his head cracked open. Thought he was dead at first. They took him over to the health center and stitched him up, but the nurse said he had severe head trauma and wasn't sure he'd even come out of his coma. When he did, he wasn't able to communicate properly. Nurse said it was Aphasia. Said he needed speech and language therapy but there's no one left to give it to him. I look after him now, since everyone left."

"Where'd everyone go?" Marc asked.

"Well, don't rightfully know. We got word the Scavs had been hitting every town from Jacksonburg to Fulton before they got here. Some survivors wanted to go north toward Lake Placid or Potsdam but others argued against it, believing the Scavs came from the north."

"What are you talking about? What are Scavs?" Logan asked, needing clarification.

"Scavengers. That's what some of the townspeople started calling them," Principal Weiss explained. "There was a horde of them. Like a huge trucker gang. Came in right after Thanksgiving. The home guard and the police tried to stop them, but didn't do any good. Well, wasn't much of them to fight the Scavs anyway. Not after we got hit really bad with the third wave of RSV. Then they took almost everything with them, including some people. They burned the town, too, on their way out. A week after, that's when most of the town's residents decided to find a safer place. Only a few of us left here now."

"You got to know where everyone went," Benny demanded. "Where are my parents?"

"And mine? What happened to them?" Marc asked.

"I don't know," she said. "Some died from the pandemic, some died at the hands of the Scavs. The rest just left. I don't know about your families. I'm sorry. Now I got to go. Jim can't keep standing in the street with no shoes on."

As Principal Weiss walked away with Jim in tow, she turned back and shouted, "Walton. Try Walton. I know a few went there."

Walton it was, just like they had originally thought.

Logan was back in the Puma, standing in the commander's hatch. He had changed his mind about taking the southern route that would lead his team through a few of the smaller towns. The route was quicker and simpler to get them to the Bridge Street bridge that crossed over the West Branch Delaware River, which would lead to the Territorial Guard base, except it also bypassed the northern section of Walton.

Knowing that some Delhi refugees had headed to Walton, Logan decided to use an alternate course that would take them through the center of northern Walton. He hoped if the townspeople saw the Republic fighting vehicles with its colors flying, it would relieve any fears about their arrival. Logan's plan was to go to the Walton Police Department first, before heading to the military installation. Someone at the Walton PD would certainly know where the Delhi expatriates had relocated.

The village of Walton may have encompassed a mere 1.6 square miles compared to Delhi's 64.60 square miles, but it had twice the population of full-time residents. That was not what Logan discovered upon their arrival, the town had been abandoned. The businesses had all been ransacked and emptied. A few of them were burnt out. The Walton PD was non-existent and looted, as well. It wasn't an encouraging start but perhaps the Territorial Guard base would have some answers.

As they turned onto Bridge Street, heading south, it took them only a moment before they saw the far side of the bridge ahead had been obstructed. Two large school buses parked nose-to-nose were intentionally positioned across the road. Through binoculars, Logan looked across the bridge to the bus barricade. There was movement inside the vehicles. He could also see the occupants were armed.

The team wasn't going to take any chances; they launched the drone to see what was beyond the barrier. It looked like a band of survivors, possibly townsfolk, but none of those they observed were people who were familiar to them. With the drone now stowed, Logan decided to investigate further. His two fighting vehicles moved side-by-side, as they cautiously proceeded across the bridge; stopping 20 yards from the busses.

Slowly rising out of the Puma's commander's hatch and onto the roof of the drive module with his hands above his head, Logan announced, "I'm First Sergeant Ross, Army of the Territorial Republic, Free District of New York, Delaware Brigade. We're not here to harm anyone. We're just looking for anyone who could tell us if any refugees from Delhi are here?"

Logan could see at least six rifle barrels protruding from the busses' windows. A woman came up through a roof hatch on the left bus armed with a shotgun. She demanded, "Prove it!"

Logan questioned, "Prove what, exactly?"

"That you're not here to do us harm!" she said as she moved more center.

Logan thought he recognized the young woman standing atop the bus's roof. He was certain he went to high school with her, but the name just wouldn't come to him.

"For a start, we could have come in guns blazing and pushed the busses out of the way. But here I am, standing out here all exposed with no weapon."

"That's a good idea," the shotgun toting woman agreed. "Take off your armor, your shirt, and that cap. Let's see if you really are unarmed."

Logan didn't hesitate. He peeled of his armored vest; then his cap and shirt. He wasn't quite bare chested. He was still wearing his A-shirt. As Logan had been undressing, he noticed the woman say something into the radio she pulled from a hip pouch. Logan was certain it was to call for reinforcements.

She gestured with her shotgun and then told him, "Now drop the pants."

"Seriously?" Logan commented. He shook his head with dissatisfaction but dropped his pants as requested. He looked back up to study the woman and said, "Satisfied or should I twirl?" with intentional snark.

"Turn around," she directed. When she was satisfied, she told him to face her with his hands in the air.

Logan now remembered her name. It had been the pixie bob haircut and four years since he had seen her that had thrown him off.

"Katie Troy," he said loudly.

The young woman returned, "What about her?"

"We were in high school together," he said, hoping to refresh her memory.

"I don't know you," she affirmed, which was a lie. Katie knew well who he was.

"Yeah, I heard that a lot in school. But you lived on Mill Street in Hamden. In the old stone house. Your father worked for the Delhi PD."

"Most people knew that," she told him.

"Okay, fair 'nough. You were our class chairperson at Delaware Academy. In freshman year, you started dating one of the Truesdell brothers." Logan looked at Katie, but she said nothing. "That's all I got. So, can I pull up my pants now?"

Katie gestured with her shotgun to do so. As he was buckling up, another young woman joined her. She was lean, muscular and sporting an undercut detached red mohawk cyberpunk haircut.

The two women exchanged a few words, and then the cyberpunk woman departed.

Katie told Logan, "You're free to enter. But just you."

The Stockton Avenue Armory also known as The Second Walton Armory (33rd Separate Company) stood on the south side of Stockton Avenue, and to the right of the south end of the bridge. The massive brick building in a late Victorian castellated style with rough-hewn limestone trim was called the Second Walton Armory, because the first had been located in the lot to its east. That building had been built and occupied in 1886, until 1896, by the 33rd Separate Company. After being vacated it was then converted for use as a school and a Grange hall. Named the Walton Grange #1454, the landmark building still stood and had been last used as a green marketplace.

Katie Troy was escorting Logan, and Logan had assumed he was being taken to the armory to be presented to the survival camp's leader. The Stockton Avenue Armory had many uses over its long life. The armory throughout the years had retained its integrity in terms of its design, setting, materials, workmanship, and feeling. The landmark building had gone under a thorough renovation nearly 50 years prior, and some modernization less than 20 years ago, when it was turned into a museum and event space. It was a perfect strategical building for defense, and weapons and munition storage. That was probably the reason Katie did not take him to it. Instead, she delivered him to an adjacent three-story home built in 1873.

Logan was surprised by who answered Katie's knock upon the residence door. It was Luci Miranda, Jessica's mother. He immediately took off his patrol hat, and said, "Ma'am. It's a pleasure to see you again."

"Hello, Logan. Please come in," she requested, with a warm and inviting smile. "Glad to see you made it home. Well, at least made it back."

Entering Logan asked, "Yes, ma'am, about that. Do you know what—"

"I know you have a lot of questions. Everything will be explained," she assured him, "if you just follow me."

Luci took him to the den. Sitting at a desk with her back to Logan was the cyberpunk girl.

"Well, I'll leave you two alone," Luci announced. "I'm sure you both have a lot to talk about."

When the young woman turned around, Logan finally got a good look at her. It was Jessica. Logan had thought about what he would say and in what order he would say it quite often, when he re-united with Jessica. His plan fell apart the moment he saw her. He was anxious. He began to unconsciously fidget with the bracelet she had given him.

With a tentative smile he said, "You've grown. I like the new hair style. It's very you."

"Compliments are cheap," she shot at him.

Her jab was like a sharp nail to the heart. He had never known her to be mean, purposely or unintentionally. Jessica had a reason. She was pissed at him. The war had ended over four months ago. She hadn't received a letter from him for nearly two years. The last she knew about him was what she had read in the local newspaper about his heroic exploits during the Battle of Dubuque. For all she knew he had just stopped caring about her at that point or was dead. Seeing him made her angry—angry enough to punch him in the face for his disregard for her feelings. Then again, she had seen the bracelet she had made him still wrapped around his wrist. This made her want to grab hold of him and give him a loving kiss. She refused to allow either feeling to control her, so she remained indifferent.

"What you said to me the day I left. Did you mean it?" he asked.

"Is that why you've come all this way? Well, maybe I did. I was just a stupid little girl in those days. Not anymore, Logan. Not me."

"Then what you whispered in my ear...?" he probed, needing to know if she still cared for him.

Logan didn't really expect to come back and find Jessica waiting to be swept into his finely toned arms and carried to a bedroom, where she would fulfill her promise to him. Nearly five years had passed since she made her middle school admission. Logan knew full well that she probably had made it as an incentive for him to come back alive, though he did hope that she still cared for him and wanted to rekindle their close relationship, and possibly more.

"Which part? It was pretty clear you forgot about what I said. You stopped writing and the war has been over for a long time," she reminded him. She then gave him another raw emotional punch. "So, I made myself stop thinking about you."

"You've changed," he said, a reflection of disappointment in his tone to her harshness.

"Have I?"

"You've always been tough on the outside but always had a warm heart. At least toward me. Now you're just cold all the way through, and to me that's a great loss."

"And what about you, running off to play war hero? Are you still the same person after all the killing?"

He admitted, "You're right. I apologize. I guess the war has scarred both of us. For that, I am whole-heartedly sorry."

"Is that all you've come for, your own selfish needs?"

Logan realized Jessica's heart had grown hard toward him. His hope for a joyous reunion with her was shattered. He also knew in part it was his own doing for not writing. So, he put his feelings for her aside, and got down to business.

"Sergeants Benny Lee and Marc Romano have come back with me, they haven't been able to find their families. We lost Sergeant David George on the way home. I'd like to tell his folks where we buried him. Do you know what happened to everyone?"

Embittered she returned, "All I know is you left. And people died because of it."

He questioned her odd remark, "And how is that?"

Jessica unleashed her spiteful, pent up anger onto him. "Because instead of joining the Home Guard, you went off to war, leaving its protection to people like my father who was disabled, and a hundred others who had no business fighting—and they died. Died because of selfish, glory-seeking little boys like you and all the others who dropped out of school to join the Territorial Guard."

Jessica's words were both venomous and untrue. The four were not glory seeking boys. They joined the military out of duty to country and to reach for the best in themselves and each other. Many of Logan's ancestors had done the same, including his uncle who died in service to his country in the Battle of Prudhoe Bay, Alaska.

Saddened by the news, Logan replied, "I'm truly sorry to hear about your father. He was a kind-hearted man... I found two grave markers in my backyard with the names of my parents. Do you know how they died?"

"I do. They were murdered," she frankly told him, and then revealed, "Murdered trying to save me and my mom from the Scavs."

"That's the second time I've heard that name," Logan said. "Who are they, and what happened?"

Jessica explained to him that shortly after the bombs fell, a large group of marauders arrived. With diminished Home Guard personnel and depleted law enforcement due to the third wave of the disease, the marauders didn't have much resistance in their efforts to pillage and destroy the town.

"They took what little we had and killed anyone that tried to stop them. If that wasn't horrible enough, then they burned down most of the town out of spite, making sure we had nothing left. It wasn't just our town they raided; it was every town to the north. We even got word that Fulton was raided, too."

She went on to tell him that the group arrived in mostly pickup trucks and cargo vans but none of their vehicles had any distinguishing markings or even license plates to identify where the group had come from.

Concealing their place of origin and a scorched-earth policy sounded to Logan like a well-organized and well thought out attack by paramilitary forces, perhaps pro-UTA partisan guerillas, who refused to give up their cause.

Logan broached the subject of his parents' deaths again. "And what of my parents?" Logan asked. "How were they killed?"

"If it weren't for them, we'd be dead or worse."

For reasons unknown, the "Scavs," as Jessica had named them, had targeted her. It would have been understandable if she had been involved in something substantial that would have marked her as a possible threat to the raiders. She had not. At least she believed she had not. Admittedly, she had taken an active role in humanitarian efforts with organizing food drives for those in need and volunteering at the community hospital. Those acts shouldn't have been flagged or deemed problematic to be placed on some evil hit list.

Jessica had been in town when the raiders came. She got wind that the invading party was looking for her. She managed to get out of the community unseen and headed home, hoping to warn her mother in case they came looking for her there. Cellphone service was very unreliable since the war and she could not get to a landline easily. Her best option was to go home. Jessica was there only a few minutes when the house phone rang. Someone in town called to warn them that some people were headed to them, and would be there any moment.

In a panic to leave, Jessica hit the wooden mailbox post at the end of the driveway as they made a hasty exit, which caused some sizable wood splinters to pierce the radiator. The Ford Bronco had made it a quarter mile down the road, when the radiator leaked out and the vehicle died. Jessica knew of only one place she and Luci could go to for help, and that was the nearby Ross residence.

Hogan and Rachel Ross were both at home. Hogan had been in the driveway washing down their horse trailer, when Luci and Jessica frantically ran up to him and explained why they needed his help. Hogan thought it best they keep off the roads. Instead, he told them it was best if they travelled by horseback through the Ross family back acreage to a small cabin that he and Logan had built when Logan was 13 years old. The cabin, which Logan called Ft. Ross, was of a fairly good size. It was equipped with solar power that supplied electricity to a small refrigerator, a small stove, and a water pump. Best of all it was in a secluded, densely treed part of the property. All they had to do was follow the remainder of the driveway. It would take them across the shallow river to their back property. Once they got across the river, they needed to abandon the dirt tractor road that led to the fields by going straight, then follow the footpath deep into the wooded area. If they kept on the pathway at a steady pace, they should reach Ft. Ross in under 20 minutes. It would make a good hide out until their pursuers abandoned their search.

"I don't know how they knew to look for me at your home, but they came just as your father nearly finished saddling the horses. He tried to stall them while mom and I finished up. We heard gunshots. Then we bolted from the barn and headed the way your father said to go. I looked back and saw him on the ground.

We just got across the river when the horse I was riding got shot out from under me. Luckily, I fell clear and was able to get onto mom's horse. Thankfully the path was narrow, so no one followed. We waited three days at the cabin. When we got back, we found your mother dead, too. She was slumped over your father with three shots in her back. Mom and I buried them, then let your horses free.

A few days after, there was a town meeting held at the university. Most people decided it was best to just leave, find a safer place. There was talk of going north but there was disagreement if it was safe. A group went north, anyway. Others didn't agree, so we came here."

"Why didn't you go to Buffalo?"

Puzzled by Logan's random question, Jessica asked, *"Buffalo? Why Buffalo?"*

"I was told that Buffalo wasn't bombed and they were taking in refugees."

"Where'd ya hear that?"

"Oddly enough, a sailor. He told us that his ship picked up a broadcast on several civilian channels reportedly from Buffalo. Stated the city and surrounding area was safe and would take in anyone that needed safe haven."

"We didn't hear that. It sounds too good to be true. You know what they say about that…"

Logan thanked her for her kindness at burying his parents, and then turned his concern to his beloved dog. "Do you know what happened to Blaze?"

To his relief, she did. There were many more questions on Logan's mind but he had been away from his team for a long time. The most important remaining question was what happened to the other team member's loved ones.

Jessica knew that Mr. Lee had died because of a mutated strain of the virus, which the vaccine and antiretrovirals were ineffective on. She didn't know about Benny's mother. Marc Romano's father died at the hands of the Scavs, having been part of the Home Guard. She didn't know anything about his mother either, as she did not know about the Lawler family. As for the George family, she only knew of one refugee with that last name, a woman. She gave Logan the address. Logan thanked her for the information. As he turned toward the door, Jessica asked him if they needed a place to layover before continuing on. He told her no, that they needed to report to the recruiting base to report in. Jessica told him it wasn't there any longer.

"I mean it's still standing" she said, "but they pulled out three years into the war. They called it an asset relocation."

Since the convoy had no place to go immediately, Logan said he would let the team know about her offer. He also told her that they had some food supplies that they could donate to the town, if she was in need. Jessica was still disagreeable toward him. She told him she didn't need his misplaced charity, and that the community had done fine without any outside help.

Logan was sure that her protest, instead of a simple "no, thank you," was said out of her anger toward him, except he wasn't going to let Jessica's resentment be the catalyst for her shortsightedness. He politely replied, "The aid was simply meant as an offer to help your community the only way I'm able, and as a thank you for the information on Benny's and Marc's families. I apologize if you thought it was meant as an insult to your ability to provide for your people or a threat to your leadership. The offer is open if you change your mind, if not, I'm sure I can find another community that would be in need."

Jessica wanted Logan to be confrontational, so she could unleash more of her contempt and infuriation with him in a verbal exchange. Logan, however, was being courteous and tolerant, and his kindness and generosity made her realize why she had cared for him so deeply in the first place. It also made her recognize she was acting like a petulant child by rebuking his charity.

She quickly replied, "Well, since you don't seem to need it, I'm sure we could put it to use."

Her words didn't come out the way they should have, and Jessica realized it a second after she said them. She should have shown gratitude for the gift with a thank you, and now with it said and Logan already out of the room, it was too late. She thought about it for a moment, and then decided perhaps it wasn't too late. She could catch Logan and thank him before he left the house. As she moved to the living room, she saw Logan speaking to her mother. She heard his words to Luci and decided it was best not to interrupt. She returned to the den.

Logan hadn't left straight away because there were two pressing matters that he needed to speak to Mrs. Miranda about. The first was two-fold. He gave her his heartfelt condolences in regard to the loss of her husband and gratitude for her kindness in helping to bury his parents. Then there was Blaze. Luci and Jessica had found Blaze in the Logan's house when they returned to the home. They had kept the good-natured, loveable canine and brought him with them. Blaze was on the back porch enjoying the spring day.

Logan wasn't sure if Blaze would remember him. After all, he had only had her for about two years before he went off to war. Blaze remembered. He was so happy to see his master again that the canine couldn't contain his excitement. After ample licking of Logan's face, he rolled onto his back so Logan good give him a generous belly rub like he used to do. The reunion between Logan and Blaze was so emotionally beautiful that Luci began to tear up. Teary eyed, too, was Logan, who rose and gave Luci a final emotional thank you for saving his beloved dog.

Luci had heard most of Jessica's conversation with Logan. She was particularly upset over one thing her daughter had led Logan to believe. It had to do with Jessica's father, Henry. She gave her daughter a verbal lashing over it.

"Shame on you, Jessica, for lying to that boy."

"I don't know what you're talking about mom," Jessica feigned, believing her mother was referring to Jessica's lie in regard to forgetting about Logan.

"Well, then, let me tell you why I'm upset with you, so you clearly understand what you said is totally unacceptable. You let Logan believe that it was his fault your dad died, when you know that's not true. You made him feel guilt over it, and that's just... just, not right and not the way I raised you to be. You need to tell him the truth and apologize for your deception."

Jessica had been dishonest in a mean-spirited way. In truth her father had died from RSV-47.d over a year prior. She also knew her intentional act was done out of spitefulness. Her mother was correct on both accounts. It was wrong to lay guilt on Logan for something he had nothing to do with and Jessica owed him an apology. Logan had been so gallant, polite and apologetic that it had infuriated her even more than she already had been with him.

"You're right," she said with deep regret. "It was wrong of me, and it's not how you raised me."

"So, you're still angry for him leaving you and then not writing?"

"No. Why should I be?"

"Because he broke your heart and you're still in love with him."

Jessica dismissed her mother's supposition. "Mom, don't be ridiculous. In love with *him?* Never."

"Horse shit!" Luci exclaimed, rebuking her new lie.

"*Mom!?* That's really wrong coming out of you."

Except, Luci was right and she told her daughter so. "Jessica Amy Miranda. You've been in love with that boy since middle school. So, stop denying it."

Jessica had never heard her mother call her by her full name. She felt like she was a child being severely scolded.

"I'm not denying it. I may have liked him as a friend long ago, but never love."

"Oh, really? Then let me tell you what I saw between the both of you, as you were growing up." Luci began enlightening her daughter with undeniable facts. "Before Logan, you were very introverted and constantly unhappy, barely cracking a smile. And no friends. That was until you started waiting at the bus shelter with him. Within months you seemed to blossom, came out of your shell, started smiling, were happy. By mid-school year, Logan started coming over under the guise of seeing if Henry needed help with anything, when your father and I knew very well it was really to see you. You always ran to the door knowing when it was him."

Jessica tried to counter but Luci stopped her, raising an index finger, letting her daughter know she was not going to let her interrupt.

"Then there was that incident with that Madanello boy at school. Remember that? Then there was your need to ride the bus every school day, even when the weather was bad. Always refusing a ride from us to school. Most of all, we knew you were in love with him when you disregarded our rule about chocolate. Every Friday he would bring you those Teardops."

With astonishment, Jessica said, "You knew about that? How?"

"I'm your mother, that's how."

"Why didn't you ever punish me over it?" she asked.

"Because we saw what a wonderful relationship you developed with Logan and your father and I approved. We weren't going to punish you for the only thing you have ever did against our wishes. Not after seeing you so happy."

Jessica was flabbergasted at all of her mother's observations; then again, Luci had always been astute. Nonetheless this didn't explain how Luci came to the conclusion she was in love with Logan.

"Okay, so Logan and I were close, granted," she admitted but it was all she was willing to confess. "But to say I was in love with him?"

"*Still* in love," Luci corrected. "Because after he left, you stayed in your room for three days crying, and kept playing that song that he and his friend Benny recorded for you over and over again. Then when his letters started to arrive, you were always the first to the mailbox. When they stopped, you were decisively different. You lost that cheerfulness you once had. But most of all it was your coldness toward him and lies you told him earlier, about your father and forgetting about him. You're so angry at him because you feel he abandoned and betrayed your relationship. That's why I know you're still love with him, and why you know it too. Now you go find him, apologize, and ask him for his help in saving what's left of this town."

"Were you standing by the door all that time?"

"Of course, I was," Luci freely admitted. "I'm your mother. That's what mothers do, look out for their children and set them straight when necessary."

Logan had come to the end of his journey. Everything that needed to be done in Walton had been accomplished. The food supplies had been stored in the Grange building, Mrs. George had been told about her son, Benny and Marc were informed about the status of their families, and camp had been set up in the armory parking lot. Now with the waning sun, it was time for him to go home.

He bid his teammates farewell and told them there would always be a place for them at his home, if they wanted. Benny and Marc couldn't believe their time together had come to an end. But it wasn't, Logan told them. They had made it home. It was what they set out to accomplish. Now it was time to a start living for living, instead of just trying to stay alive.

Benny offered to drive Logan home, but he declined. He wanted to walk and take in the sights and sounds of the night, to smell the rural spring air that didn't stink like diesel, spent munitions, or death. Besides, he told them. it was only a six hour walk and the moon and stars were bright enough to light his trek. Plus, he'd have Blaze for company. He was leaving fully armed, with his body armor on, his two rifles, a pistol, and plenty of ammo in his rucksack. If there was any trouble getting to Delhi, he'd be fully prepared for it.

Jessica knew she needed to go see Logan and apologize for treating him poorly and unfairly. She also wanted to privately discuss with him the current situation with the Scavs. She procrastinated for hours, unable to face him. By the time she made her way to Logan's encampment, she found he was gone. Benny tried to radio him but Logan didn't answer. Jessica left without discussing the Scav situation with anyone else. Luci told her daughter to take a few guards and go after him but Jessica wasn't about to do it. It wasn't that she didn't want to, it was that it was not wise to pull resources from patrol duty.

The Scavs had not continued south onto Walton after plundering and burning Delhi. They had left the way they had come, from the north. This had been a blessing for the residents of Walton as well as the Delhi survivors who fled south. The town welcomed Jessica and her companions, and set them up in a temporary residence inside the armory. This had been the saving grace for those who had followed Jessica.

The Village of Walton believed they were prepared to repel any invasion if it came. They had built checkpoints and barricades at key roads into the town. The Walton Home Guard, though without significant personnel, was armed with shotguns, hunting rifles, and pistols. They helped supplement the town's small police force when it came to patrolling the village.

Jessica argued with the Home Guard commander—the mayor—and the chief of police that the barricades at the checkpoints were inadequate and under staffed, especially Lower 3rd Brook Road that was shabbily barricaded and had no sentries. She highly argued for every capable resident to be armed and trained to defend the town and all the barricades be reinforced. Her strong recommendations were dismissed as youthful overreaction and post-traumatic stress at what happened in Delhi. The mayor and chief of police assured her the situation was in control and not to upset the townsfolk with her misguided worries. They both agreed that Lower 3rd Brook Road hadn't been repaired since the start of the war and was now unusable. Their limited resources were better used at more suitable entry points into the hamlet. Besides, Winter was coming. *If* the raiders came to Walton, they certainly wouldn't come until spring. The authorities were wrong.

The initial raiding party came from the north in two groups, using the two main roads into town. However, this was not their main force. The largest group came in from the west, using Lower 3rd Brook Road, just as Jessica had warned. The town's police and Home Guard were overwhelmed within minutes, and the Scavs had control of Walton within 30 minutes. In three hours, the town had been ransacked and looted, and the raiders had once again fled north leaving the town devastated with death and destruction.

For some reason, whether by divine intervention, lack of proper information on the town, or simply deeming the area insignificant— knowing the guard base had been abandoned—the Scavs had not crossed the bridge into southern Walton to pillage when they attacked in late December. Jessica had been at the armory when the invasion came. Some residents who were closest to the bridge when the destruction and killing began managed to flee across the river and to the armory. Others already on the southern side also sought safety behind the fortress walls.

The community was now only 83 people, large but not strong, when it came to those who could help defend their refuge. Of those, a quarter of the population was made up of adolescents and young children, and a few elderly. Of the able-bodied men that remained, there were only twelve. Three had been engineers at the Waste Water Treatment Plant, four from the Delaware County Hospital, one from the Walton Middle/High School, two from the metal works company, and two were original Delhi survivors. Thankfully, all but one had skills that were necessary to keep their refuge functioning. This left 50 women ranging from teenage years to early 60s. Many were assigned to farming, fishing, and caring for their livestock outside the safe zone. The remainder of the women were fighters. They guarded the safe zone night and day, either by being stationed along perimeter points on sentry duty, part of vehicle patrols, or watching over those who had to go outside the safe zone.

The safe zone was really a misnomer. Although the niche they had carved out for themselves was fairly encompassing, it was not highly defendable when it came to its borders. Certainly, the northern entrance was secure with the busses and guards, which protected the only main route from the north into southern Walton. Additionally, it had the West Branch Delaware as a further deterrent. The spring rain had kept the river high and rapid, making crossing it hazardous.

To their east and west, the river ran north to south. Again, the water was a deterrent, but when June came it would become low again. At certain points it would become shallow enough that the stone bed would be exposed making walking across it very easy. To their south, a football field's length from the southern border of the Walton Cemetery, was a dense wooded area. The forested expanse was massive enough that even all-terrain vehicles would have difficulty navigating through it, but it was not impervious enough to disregard it as a vantage point for an enemy foot incursion.

With the mayor, police department, and Home Guard unable to protect Walton's residents, and now dead, those who remained turned to Jessica for leadership. Jessica rose to the challenge. She set up an enclave within a larger territory, which tightened their living space to a more reasonable defendable area. She called this the safe zone. Inside the safe zone was the armory, the metal works shop, and the hospital. What was outside was the abandoned Territorial Guard Base, the Water Works Treatment Plant, Walton Middle/High School, and the Delaware County Fairground. The fairground was a significant location for their survival. It was where four massive vegetable gardens where being cultivated. It also housed two milk cows, three horses, and a lot of chickens in two of the exhibition buildings. Every house and business establishment in southern Walton had been scavenged. All food and sundry items were taken to the grange for storage, and all scrounged weapons and ammunition were securely locked inside the armory's arsenal. Tools were also kept in the grange building, and dispensed every morning during job assignments. It had been a lot of work but there were enough supplies gathered to get them through the summer. That was if the Scavs didn't return as they threatened.

It had happened two weeks before Logan and his team arrived. There was a group of 30 Scavs that made their way onto the bridge, but made no attempted assault. Instead, a spokesperson for the group had come with an edict. They requested to deliver their decree directly to "… the head bitch in charge, Jessica Miranda." Once again, Jessica found herself being sought out by the marauders. The young man, somewhere around the age of 20, told Jessica that if she surrendered to them, and turned over all their weapons and food, then maybe— just maybe—they wouldn't slaughter every person over the age of 12. Jessica knew they had no intention of keeping their half-assed promise. She had seen their brutality twice before, and knew they would kill anyone able to give resistance to them.

Her refusal was taken in stride but not without threat. The spokesperson told her they would return June 1st with the entire strength of their group, and if she refused to comply, she and her survival group would feel their full wrath.

Jessica had missed Logan by about two hours. No, she had told her mother, it wasn't wise to even send a couple of people out to find Logan, especially after dark. What was done was done, and if Logan chose to return one day, Jessica would give him the apology she needed to give him.

Luci, on the other hand, didn't accept her daughter's excuse. It wasn't so much that her Jessica hadn't given Logan a proper apology, as it was the fact that the Scavs would be returning. Luci knew they would be true to their threat. Although Jessica had done a fine job and was selfless in her work in building up the safe zone's defenses, Luci knew it wasn't going to be enough to prevent the Scavs from getting what they wanted. It wasn't that Luci was trying to undermine Jessica's authority or belittle everything that Jessica had accomplished, for she had done an amazing and nearly impossible job with their survival efforts. It was simply they needed help in fighting the Scavs. Luci knew that if anyone could help, it was Logan and his team. Luci went to talk with them.

"Pigheaded and foolish, and too damn proud not to ask you herself," Luci told the group, and then explained the situation. She also requested that they not reveal that she had come to them asking for aid, but it needed to be done.

Benny said he understood, but he needed to see if his mother was still alive. He needed to check a few other places that she might have taken refuge in, like a few church friends' homes or perhaps at her sister's place. Marc, too, said he wished he could help but he needed to find his girlfriend and any family. He knew there were a couple places he could look, too. In the end, only Milan said he would stay to help, since he had no family and no place to go. Plus, he was an engineer and he was certain he could be of use.

Food was running low and harvest season was months away. There was no certainty that the crops they had yet to plant would take and be fruitful. The canned goods Logan had generously donated was a help, but with all the mouths to feed it wasn't going to last very long. Jessica had no choice but to do another scrounging mission. Since they had scavenged every town within a 40-50 mile radius, they would have to travel farther in hopes of finding more supplies. Knowing Albany to the Northeast had been bombed, she thought it best not to scavenge any closer than they previously had. She had heard survivors in communities near cities that had been bombed reporting over civilian radio that the bombs turned people into goo. She had also heard rumors that those cities were still contaminated. She brought the subject up with Milan, hoping he would know fact from fiction. Milan said they had scavenged a liquor store in Phoenix shortly after the bombs had dropped, and had no ill effects from consuming the libations or being in the city. Jessica was unsure of how the community would feel about food scavenged from a rumored contaminated area, even though Milan said it was safe. The other closest large populated city was Binghamton, just under 60 miles west. Jessica hadn't heard that the city had been bombed, then again, she hadn't heard any news out of Binghamton since "The Fall," as she and others called it. There was a high probability there were survivors there, and Jessica would not be welcome. The only way to know for sure was to travel there.

There was some dissension about Jessica and her team being in charge, detractors that believed "kids" shouldn't be in control of the survival group, and that leadership was best done by adults. This, however, was not the majority sentiment amongst the community. Many felt gratitude and indebted to Jessica and her team for keeping them alive, fed, and fairly safe and secure. Jessica aimed to keep it that way by being proactive. A leader leads and therefore she led the mission to Binghamton, taking Donna Testa and Danny Troy with her.

Before the formation of The Republic, Binghamton had been a major manufacturing hub for food and beverages, electrical and electronics, sporting goods, along with a plethora of other industries. When the war began, the city boomed both figuratively and literally. Binghamton became one of the major manufacturing cities for supplying The Republic with military clothing, boots, and rucksacks. It also made viper missiles for Republic aircraft and tires for their war machines. This made Binghamton a major target for UTA air strikes. In the entirety of the civil war, there had been perhaps a dozen major ground battles. Contrastingly, bombings were common and frequent, and were the preferred method of warfare. Binghamton suffered many tactical airstrikes, both from unmanned aerial vehicles and planes that were not always precise.

Two Guys was the largest hypermarket store in the area. It was a store Jessica had visited often with her family, especially for school supplies. Besides groceries, the mega store had other important departments vital for the community's continued survival; including a gardening department and lots of clothing. However, clothing was not something they were in dire need of. Food and seeds were on the top of the list, especially baking needs, followed by toilet paper and other hygiene items. There were also two items on Jessica's private list: Ballentine Ale and Teardrops. The beer had been her father's favorite and she wanted to take a few bottles back for her mother, who also enjoyed it. The Teardrops, of course, were Logan's favorite chocolate. If she ever saw Logan again. "No," she told herself. *When* she saw Logan again, she would apologize and gift the chocolates as a peace offering. Then there was their need for weapons: bullets, rifles, pistols, knives, machetes, axes and hopefully some broadhead arrows for Donna's archery bow. Luckily, next to Two Guys was Trout's Outpost, a retailer of hunting, fishing, camping and other related outdoor recreation merchandise.

The plaza they were headed to was off the Southern Tier Expressway, aka Route 17, north of the Susquehanna River and near to the Tice & Dickman sand and gravel quarry. First, they would have to travel across the Chenango River and pass through Binghamton proper and continue west before making their exit. The drive in their Valentine Express Company rental box truck to Binghamton was uneventful, which was welcome. When they reached the outskirts of the city, the strange beauty of unkempt greenery and abandoned homes along the way took a turn as they drew closer to the city limits. At first the panorama was periodically dotted with burnt out homes, most likely attributed to neglect after The Fall. As they drew closer to the river overpasses of routes 17 and 81, the scenery began to look decisively different. At first the roadways and surrounding area appeared to be in a state of repair. The expressway was spotted with road construction equipment, seemingly abandoned in mid-restoration. Jessica assumed it was because the bridges over the river would have been another prime target of the UTA. She wondered if the bridges would even be standing let alone passable, providing they weren't barricaded and guarded by the townspeople. Danny slowed their vehicle as they approached a checkpoint at the cross over entry, but it was unused and only showed signs of dilapidation. They proceeded cautiously. As they drove across the river and into the city, the landscape became pock-marked with craters from bombs that missed their targets. Nearby homes also bore scars, all mute reminders of the horrors of a war that had only recently ended.

Jessica rolled down the passenger window. The world around them was eerily quiet. She strained to hear one bird's chatter but there was none, and she could see no birds anywhere. The unearthly stillness gave her the creeps. Nearing their exit off the expressway, they were greeted with a car jam on both the east and west bound lanes. Directly in front of the massive vehicle barricade was what appeared to be a mammoth unexploded missile. Stopping 20 or so yards from the debris field, Jessica climbed up on the roof of their box truck with her binoculars to suss out the situation.

The missile was mostly intact, though the forward warhead section was detached from the rest of the twisted body. As she studied the weapon, she saw about a two-foot-long crack in the warhead. The crack perhaps had a three-inch gape in it. Below it was a symbol. At first, she couldn't quite make it out, since the angle she was at partly obscured it. She moved left over the driver's portion of the roof to get a better look. A sick feeling rose from her stomach and into her throat. The graphic on the warhead was a biohazard symbol. Jessica moved her binoculars around the roadside. She saw unkempt bundles of discarded clothing. She knew what it meant. She was certain by the biohazard symbol on the missile that Binghamton, NY had also been a targeted city. But why hadn't the biological fallout reached Walton? she wondered. How had they been spared? Maybe the wind had blown westerly that day, sparing all the towns to the east. Except if that were true, she thought, wouldn't the contamination from the bomb dropped on Albany have blown to Walton then? She told Donna and Danny her discovery. None of them wanted to return to Walton with an empty truck. They had to re-supply.

There was no way to continue forward but Jessica knew another route, the one her father liked to use, which was back to the previous off ramp and through a residential area. There was only one car in the parking lot in front of Two Guys, and both of the vehicle's front doors were open. Investigation proved that the car had been abandoned for some time. Danny dropped Jessica and Donna off at the main entrance and drove to the loading dock at the back of the building.

The store still had a functioning solar array but many of the lights inside were no longer lit. As Donna and Jessica made their way through the store to the back of the building where they would find the entry to the loading dock, they mentally took note of the items they passed by. Though there were supplies, the selection was sparse due to both the pandemic and the war. As they moved deeper into the building the odor of spoiled fish, meat, and decayed fresh produce hung heavy in the air. Even the working refrigeration couldn't keep the items from spoiling after nearly six months.

The group had hoped to find a reasonably supplied stock room so they could quickly off load the products into the box truck, but to their disappointment there was less in the back room than on the store shelves. Both Donna and Jessica returned to the store's grocery area, retrieved shopping carts, and then gathered up as many items as possible that were on their shopping list. They continued to fill up shopping carts and delivered them to Danny at the loading dock for an hour. Jessica found the beer, but the shelves in the candy aisle were bare. With the truck half full, and little left on the store's shelves that they were in need of, they decided to move onto Trout's Outpost to see what was available.

The front wood and glass doors to the shop were secured. As Jessica peered in, the store looked reasonably stocked, at least what she could see. From the entryway, you couldn't see to the back of the store to where the hunting supplies were located. The route going back was blocked. As it was in all Trout's Outpost stores, there was a large diorama 20 feet from the entry that greeted you. You either had to take the right or left path to circle around it. The display was a lifelike manikin of American pioneer and frontiersman John Trout, dressed in buckskin clothes, head adorned with a coonskin hat, and who proudly stood with one elevated foot forward upon a rock, musket rifle in hand, and a beaver trap slung over one shoulder. He was set to a backdrop of some majestic mountains. John Trout, of course, was a fictional character, and how the character came about Jessica never bothered to investigate. To her the Daniel Boone-esque display was a bit cheesy, but it was a staple in all Trout shops.

There was no other choice but to smash in the glass of the front doors to gain access. The box truck was too tall and wide to use the backend as a battering ram, so Jessica carefully used the butt stock of her Daniel Defense DD5 V5 Hunter carbine rifle to break the window. The glass gave way easily. After clearing the frame of the remaining broken shards, Jessica reached in and unlocked the cylinder lock with its inside thumb turn. The doors had been open for about a minute when an alarm began to blare. The unexpected noise made all three of them jump from shock. No one had thought about the locked shop having an active burglar alarm.

The noise was only mildly irritating, and wasn't going to deter them from their scavenging. Danny positioned the rear of the truck toward the entry doors, while Donna went to the hunting supplies department to find some knives, tools and arrows, while Jessica moved to the shooting department to look for guns and ammo. The two departments were practically side-by-side, and both were lacking anything substantial. Every pistol and rifle display was empty, and all that remained were a few shotguns. There wasn't a lot of ammo either, three boxes of Federal Classic .45 ACP 230 grain jacketed hollow point—perfect for Donna's pistol—and nearly a dozen boxes of 9mm Luger cartridges, which was perfect Jessica's Glock 26. Except there were no .308 Winchester rounds that she needed for her carbine rifle. Jessica wasn't surprised. Self-defense weapons had been quickly bought up when the civil war began and Home Guard units were formed. Furthermore, weapons manufacturers within The Republic turned to making firearms and ammo for the military instead of civilian use. Jessica gathered and bagged the pistol ammunition, plus a dozen boxes of shotgun shells along with five box magazines for the three remaining Remington shotguns and headed for the door, never hearing the rifle shots from outside or Danny's urgent calls over her 2-way radio that had its volume set low. Donna hadn't heard Danny either, because she didn't have a radio. There wasn't an extra one to spare for the scavenging mission.

Seventeen-year-old Daniel Troy—Danny as he preferred to be called—saw them coming the moment they entered the empty parking lot. At the speed they were approaching he had no reason not to believe they were aggressive. He opened up the truck's driver door and stood behind it, using it for cover as well as to conceal the rifle he was holding. Danny grabbed his 2-way radio and called to Jessica but she didn't respond. The three vehicles came to a halt about 25 yards from him. The moment the occupants exited their vehicles they opened fire, pelting the door Danny was standing behind.

There was more than a dozen of them pushing forward, but Danny noticed there was something odd in their behavior. They moved forward seemingly with disregard for their lives. As if they were unafraid to die. Plus, they weren't even bothering to make a speedy attack. They lumbered forward as they fired but many of the shots seemed to be wild. As they drew closer Danny opened fire but he hadn't got more than a couple of burst off when his rifle jammed. "Turd-sticks," he cussed. He knew he had to do something dramatic in both evasion and to get Jessica's and Donna's attention. Danny jumped in the truck and started the ignition. As he looked out his windshield a few rounds pelted the safety glass but Danny didn't even flinch. He was too transfixed on the people coming toward him, if that's what they still could be called. They were gross looking. They looked like wax statues that had been put out under a hot summer's sun to melt. Well, perhaps that was an over exaggeration, he thought. But certainly, their skin was all droopy, like really old people with that loose skin condition. In addition, from what he could tell, they also had some open growths on their flesh which added to the gross out factor.

Another couple of rounds pelted the windshield, one just missing him, which woke him from his trance. Danny threw the truck in reverse and hit the gas. There was no way he was going to let the raiders get the supplies they had worked so hard at gathering. The truck struck the building, shaking it. It was right in a place where no one was going to be able to open the cargo doors. Danny grabbed the ignition keys and bolted into the shop.

Jessica was coming around a corner of the diorama when the

building suddenly shook. Alarmed, she dropped the supplies she was carrying and swung her Daniel Defense rifle forward that she had slung over her back, just as Danny ran in.

It didn't take long before Donna joined them, hearing the last few words of the excited warming he was giving over the still ringing alarm. "… More than a dozen."

"Are they the Scavs, Danny?" she asked with urgency. Jessica knew if they were the Scavs, the three of them wouldn't be able to put up much of a fight, being out numbered and facing superior firepower.

"No, they can't be," Danny assured her. "They're… they're, really gross looking. Like they're sick, or—"

An eruption of weapons fire shattered the two arch style windows opposite the entry doors. Then a barrage of bullets ripped through the front entry, causing the three to duck for cover on the backside of the John Trout display, just as the manikin was being shredded by bullets.

Donna asked, "Danny, where's your rifle?"

"Jammed and in the truck," he told her.

Jessica grabbed two of the discarded shotguns, two boxes of shells, and three box magazines. She handed one each to Danny. Then the three of them ran toward the back of the store just as the attackers breached the entry.

Jessica and Donna led Danny to the back of the store and into the small loading dock. Jessica told him to stay where he was no matter what, that one of them, if they survived, would come back for him. If not, then he should escape out the back door when he thought it safe.

Donna and Jessica moved to the double swing doors that divided the loading dock from the showroom, and looked out into the store. They didn't see anyone, but they were both certain the enemy was out there searching the aisles. As far as Jessica knew the attacking group didn't know how many others were with Danny. This hopefully would give them an edge. There were too many invaders in close, cluttered quarters for Donna to effectively use her bow against them. So, Jessica gave Donna the pilfered pump action Remington Model 900 DX Tactical 12-gauge shotgun. Its detachable box magazine could hold 6-rounds. They only had two and some spare shells.

Neither of them had actual killed anyone in close combat. The only fire fight they had been in was when they had escaped to the safety of the armory when the Scavs first came to Walton. Though they had exchanged weapons fire, neither knew if they had even struck any Scav. Both knew this would be a fight for their lives. The two of them nodded to one another and then watchfully moved across the threshold. Immediately one combatant came out from around the firearms display cases where Jessica had pilfered the shotguns and ammo. Donna unloaded a round into his chest. They hadn't stepped another eight feet when two more assailants came around the corner of the second aisle to their left. Jessica let loose with a barrage of .308 Winchester ammo. The .308s tore through the two. Then another came from a right aisle. Donna blasted him, and then turned to check their rear position. There was another one armed with an automatic rifle. She shot him just as he pulled his trigger. The automatic rifle he was carrying sprayed bullets into the ceiling as the man fell to the floor.

The two cautiously moved forward toward an area of clothing racks that were sandwiched in between the aisles they were leaving and the aisles ahead. As they reached the last aisle before the clothing, a woman popped up from behind it. She was face-to-face with Jessica. As the woman raised her pistol, Jessica shot her three times in the torso with the pistol she was holding in her other hand. The woman's weapon discharged though, grazing Jessica in her leg. The injury stung but it wasn't debilitating. For the moment there were no other aggressors. They both decided to change out their magazines for fully loaded ones.

It was difficult getting a fix on their enemy. That damn alarm was still going off, so all they had was line of sight. Then again, the noise would also mask their footfalls, especially Jessica's heavy combat boots. Neither of them had actually paused to take a look at who was attacking them. That was until that moment. Looking at the corpse of the aggressor Jessica had just killed, they saw the extent of the sickness that Danny had been trying to convey. The corpse had a severe case of elastosis accompanied by some sort of keratoacanthomas. At least that is how Jessica's mother would have phrased it. The loss of skin elasticity was horrible enough but the skin growths that were oozing some sort of dayglow yellow pus and bleeding reddish purple blood was truly gross. If that wasn't disgusting enough, the same fluorescent yellow pus was excreting from the woman's left nostril, and the iris of her left eye had turned blood red.

"Damn," Donna whispered. "Do you think that is from those bombs that were dropped?"

"I don't know," Jessica returned. "Maybe. I just hope they're not toxic." Jessica signaled for Donna to continue up the path they were on toward the front, while she went to the right toward the other main path. They would meet where the two paths met, in front of the John Trout diorama.

Jessica was the first to get to the rendezvous point, she immediately opened fire, laying down a spray of bullets at the five that were gathered in the main entry area. Donna was only five seconds behind. She arrived just in time as another five aggressors rushed through the entry doors. A hail of shotgun blasts and .308 rounds tore the enemy apart before they could make it more than eight feet into the shop. Both women dropped their weapons and grabbed for their pistols, expecting more to come through the door or come from behind. But there were no more.

Then three shotgun blasts rang out over the alarm. *Danny!* They both believed. They hurried with caution to where they left him.

Carefully peeking through the windows of the double swinging traffic doors, they saw Danny with his back toward them, facing a rear exit door next to the loading dock pull down door.

"Danny!" Jessica shouted, as they slowly came through the doors. Danny turned to face them. He had a look of dread on his face.

"Someone was trying to ram the door down, he explained. "I didn't have a choice."

The exit door was peppered with bb shot.

Jessica and Donna both embraced Danny to give him comfort. But as quickly as they put their arms around him, he violently rejected their act. Danny pushed away from them as he simultaneously pumped the shotgun he held to load another shell in the chamber. Before either woman knew what was happening, Danny let loose with a blast at someone coming through the double doors. The assailant with the automatic rifle fell back across the archway propping the doors open. Danny dropped his weapon. The color drained from his face. Clutching his abdomen, he collapsed to his knees... then he vomited; three times. It was the first time he had knowingly killed someone.

Afterward the three of them swept the entire store together making sure there were no more combatants inside or outside. When they were sure, they gathered up what they needed and headed to the truck. Jessica made sure to go to the Boating Department where the portable 2-way radios were located. She found five.

There wasn't a great deal of talking on the way back to Walton, with exception to keeping their discovery to the upper echelon. Sure, there would be talk from the townsfolk about the shot-up box truck. However, there was nothing to gain by letting the community know that the hostiles they encountered were sick. It would only panic them. At least they knew that the city was still inhabited. There were certainly more stores in Binghamton they could scrounge from but they would have to weigh the risk against the reward at a later date with the survivor committee. Certainly, if they chose to return, they'd have to bring a few more people with them, who they could trust, and who were also good combatants. For now, they had enough supplies for an additional three weeks.

PART IV

STRINGMAN

THERE WAS A LOT OF WORK TO BE DONE, LOGAN KNEW, IF HE WAS going to get his home back up to living standards. He would have to till the back acreage and plant the hay for the horses. He would also have to till and plant the vegetable garden his mother made each year. Mostly she had grown small crops of corn, cucumbers, carrots, and radishes.

The horse barn needed cleaning and some minor repair. He needed to bring down hay from the loft. He would also have to get the two remaining horses back in their coral, trim their hoofs, and give them a much-needed grooming. He had to take account of the family emergency supplies that were stored in the basement/root cellar. Then there were the Miranda's hundreds of chickens. They were running all over the place—in the street, on his property, and on the Miranda property. He could construct a coup and pen for them. He could have fresh eggs and fresh poultry when he wanted. He also knew he would have to go to his father's shop and bring back every last bag of horse and chicken feed to the family farm. Plus, he needed to retrieve any ammunition that might remain at Ross & Reynolds. He could use it with the family guns. He couldn't forget about Blaze. All that was left at home was an air tight ten pound container of dry dog chow and a few cans of wet. He hoped there was still some at Ross & Reynolds. If not, Blaze would be eating a lot of chicken. If he was headed into town, he'd certainly want to stop off and see Jim Reynolds.

The first thing on his to do list was go look at the horse Jessica had been riding. He was already upset before he and Blaze got to where Jessica said she abandoned the dead animal. The Ross's only had three horses, one for each family member. The ones that belonged to his mother and father had been accounted for. This meant that Jessica had been riding Frost, Logan's white mare. There wasn't much left of his beloved mare when he came across her. Scavenger animals had devoured most of her. What was left was now being consumed by maggots. There was no salvaging the saddle. The weather and animal decomposition had destroyed it.

It was Logan's birthday. He was 22-years-old today. This, however, was not a day he wished to celebrate. His reunion with Jessica a week prior had left him feeling rejected and a bit unwanted. This coupled with the loss of his family and absent friends caused him to feel unloved and alone. He attempted to bury his thoughts and emotions by going about his daily chores as usual, but it wasn't cathartic. So, he tried to relieve his depression and anxiety by practicing his quick draw and target acquisition with his replica 1873 .45 caliber Colt Single Action Army Revolver, better known as a Peacemaker. He followed this with some target practice with his father's replica Winchester Model 1873 repeating rifle. Both Ross men were very fond of old American and Italian Western films, especially those of Clint Eastwood, Randolph Scott, George Eastman, Gianni Garko, and Anthony Stefan, to name a few. Neither of these did anything to ease his troubled mind. He soon returned to his chores.

Two hours before sundown, Logan was sitting in a chair on the front porch with a bottle of bourbon to one side of him and his Peacemaker over the back of the chair to his other side. Nearby was his father's Winchester rifle. And of course, by his feet was Blaze, who was chewing on a large dog treat.

Logan was on the front porch doing what he loved to do best, playing guitar. He had spent an hour performing a bunch of Neil Young, Grateful Dead, West of Hell, Blue Rodeo, Due North, and Ron Hawkins songs to temper his foul mood. Logan was a huge fan of artists that combined folk, rock, country and other musical styles. It was one of the reasons he formed the roots rock band The Bruce Lees with Benny and the two Davids. They all had a love of the same style of music. Nonetheless, playing folk/rock/country was not Logan's first love in music. His first music choice was blues. Admittedly though, he was not a prodigy at it, like his uncle had been.

After he set his Gibson acoustic down next to his D'Angelico Excel EXL-1 Throwback Archtop Hollow Body electric guitar, and removed the harmonica rig around his neck, he wasn't sure which electric guitar to play next. He did know he was now in the temperament to perform some blues music.

His three guitars were very precious to him. They had all belonged to the uncle he had never known, who had died in the War for Alaska.

His father's brother, Uncle Sheridan had been in a blues cover band before joining the military, and could play guitar as easily as a songbird could croon. Logan's father had given him Sheridan's guitars and some digital music recordings of Sheridan to Logan on his 13th birthday. He hemmed and hawed for a moment whether to pick up his D'Angelico or his Holgado. In the end, he chose the Telecaster since he hadn't played it, yet. The Telecaster was handmade by Tomas Holgado at Holgado Guitar Works in 2018. It had been created from salvaged lumber pulled from the walls, floors, and railings of the former original site of the Masquerade Theatre in Atlanta, GA. He plugged it into his practice amp and began to play "Homesick" by Marcus King—the first blues song he ever learned, having been one of his uncle's favorite artists. The Holgado Telecaster could cry the blues so sweetly.

He was barely through the five-minute song when a tactical war machine came down his driveway. He grabbed his father's rifle that was leaned up against the house but then returned to his playing as soon as he saw who it was. It was most of his team, both new and old. And there was Lisa with Marc.

Approaching, Kristen was astonished by Logan's performance. "*Wow!* I had no idea you could play and sing. That's amazing," she added.

As Logan continued to lay down some serious guitar licks, he head gestured to Benny and remarked, "Not only me," letting her know Benny had talent too. Looking up at Kristen, Logan spontaneously changed the last two lines of the song and sang, "Kristen's the only one. Lord, she's the only one that keeps Benny from staying gone." Having finished, he set his guitar onto its stand and finally greeted them. "Well, well, well, look at all of you, and Lisa, too," Logan welcomed everyone with a hug. "Aren't we missing someone and a truck?"

"The Chief is still in Walton as far as we know, along with the HGC we parked inside the armory," Benny replied.

"So, it looks like the three of you didn't stay, either," Logan observed.

"Nope, as you can see," Marc answered. "We've been searching for family this past week."

"Well, you found Lisa. That's a good thing. Anyone else?"

Benny shook his head. "No luck finding my mom or aunt but Marc found his mother, Lisa and her mom down in Roscoe."

"You mean the old campsite your family used to go to every year?" Logan directed at Marc.

"Yeah. Bunch of survivors there but the town is completely abandoned."

"So, what are you all doing here?" Logan asked, puzzled as why they would comeback.

Benny replied, "We came to check on you, birthday boy."

"Seriously?" he said with a slight tone of disbelief.

Benny smiled and asked, "So, how you doing?"

Though Benny's words were sincere, Logan could see they were also a thinly disguised opening remark meant as a lead in for something else. He humored Benny, anyway. "Awesome. Took the day off. Got up at 8 a.m., had a big pile of eggs, did some practice shooting with the Peacemaker and Winchester... Ah, fed the horses, fed the chickens. Took a dump, showered, shaved, and then been playing guitar and hanging out with Blaze... Now what's really on your mind?"

"What's the matter?" Benny asked. "Can't we come and check in on our commander and friend on his birthday to see how he's doing without an ulterior motive?"

"First, it's *former* commander," Logan reminded them. "And second I don't see any presents or birthday cake, which is probably a good thing 'cause I know none of you losers know how to bake," he jokingly said. "So, doc, you want to tell me what you're all really doing here?"

"Well for one, we're out of food," Kristen began. "We gave all our MREs to the survivors at the campsite. So, we thought you'd like to go for a supply run. Second... Benny should tell you the other reason."

"*Benny?*" Logan questioned with suspicion.

"Well, okay," Benny began, giving in. "It's not all about your birthday and our lack of food. We were kinda feeling guilty about leaving Walton after Mrs. Miranda came to see us, so we thought we'd go get the Chief, and then go get the Two Guys truck."

"And what did Mrs. Miranda say to make you feel guilty?"

Benny reluctantly explained. "Well, after Jessica came looking for you—"

"To unleash more anger at me I suppose."

"—Mrs. Miranda paid us a visit and told us the Scavs came a couple weeks before we got there. She said they were looking for Jessica, and it wasn't the first time. They told Jessica that they would be back by June 1st, and that if she didn't surrender to them, they'd kill everyone."

"*And?*" Logan questioned.

Kristen interjected, "So, we all thought we'd come and get you to help defend Walton when they came. Their defenses frankly suck donkey balls. They'll be slaughtered."

"Even if I wanted to go, my schedule won't allow it," Logan began "Too much to do around here. Feed the chickens, shovel horse shit, wallow in self-pity, wrestle with my self-disgust. And I can't forget dinner with me. I won't call that off again. Totally booked!" Logan told them, dryly.

"After all that trouble we encountered getting home and seeing what the Scavs did to Delhi, you're just going to sit here like you don't care?" Benny asked with a bit of disbelief and outrage.

"Look, we just spent four plus years in the Army, following orders and chasing the enemy. But this one's not my job, not my fight, and not my business."

"Whaddya tawkin' about?! Liaaaaah. Stop pretending you don't care and get up off your ass," Kristen demanded.

"Listen, all of you. I'm tired of the fighting, the killing, and getting shot at. I don't want to be that Logan anymore," he told them. "Consider him dead."

"You want to talk about dead?" Benny asked him. "I'm calling in your IOU."

Logan pretended ignorance. "I have no idea what you're talking about."

"You're going to go down that road?" Benny asked. "Well, then. Battle of Chambersburg. What did you tell me after I saved your ass?"

Logan knew what he had promised but he didn't want to acknowledge it. If he did, he knew he'd have to do whatever Benny requested. Logan was certain of what Benny was going to ask him to do, and he didn't like it.

"I think I shit myself?" Logan returned with a smart aleck reply.

"Don't be an asshat. Say it."

"No," Logan refused. "Not for this. Just let it go."

Logan had never backed down from a fight and was definitely acting out of character. Benny knew the truth to why Logan didn't want to help. Benny called him out on it.

"Let's face it, Logan. This has nothing to do with you not wanting to help, and everything to do with your bruised ego," Benny unequivocally told him. "We heard how your reunion with Jessica went. You're just pissed and hurt because she didn't come begging for your help. Well, according to Mrs. Miranda that's why Jessica came looking for you. But you would have known that if you hadn't bailed. So, stop embarrassing yourself in front of all your friends and suck it up," he decreed.

Benny had been correct about everything and it irked Logan even more. It was not because Benny had bitch-slapped him with the truth. After all, Benny was his closest friend, and that's what true friends do —call you out and set you straight when you're being an *asshat*. What was irritating him was two-fold. First, he had decided to deal with the "Jessica situation" by not dealing with it at all and by leaving, having "bailed" as Benny had reminded him. Secondly, if Jessica truly had wanted his help, why didn't she make an effort by at least sending an emissary to fetch him? He felt slighted by her inaction. Then again, he realized he was being petty and immature, and all the anger and hurt he was feeling was actually self-inflicted. Benny was right when he had told Logan to suck it up.

"*Asshat?* You called me an asshat," Logan sighed.

"That's what you took away from this entire conversation?" Benny asked.

"So, who's going to take care of the farm while I'm away?" Logan asked, letting the team know he was onboard.

Lisa came forward with a hand raised, volunteering. "I can. If you're alright with that."

"There'll be a list," Logan warned.

Logan half expected the Two Guys truck to either be gone or to have been looted. The team was glad it was still there and unpilfered. On their way back from Southfields, NY, they stopped off at C E Kiff in Delhi to refuel before returning to Walton.

Logan had no intention of telling Jessica they needed Milan and their HGC to go fetch a tractor trailer. All he said to her was that Chief Crncevic and the HGC were mission critical for what they needed to do. He also didn't bother to tell her they were coming back either. When Jessica pressed him for a reason why, all he would tell her was the more he had thought about what she had told him about the Scavs looking for her a second time raised his suspicions. It was possible she may have a spy amongst her group. It was better to err on the side of caution than to reveal any aspects of where they were headed or what their objective was.

The team couldn't hide the fact they were bringing a tractor trailer back through the bridge barricade and to the armory parking lot. News travelled fast. Some came to look but Logan had given orders to his team that no one outside their crew was to get near it or reveal the contents of what was inside.

One in particular, Marc would later report to Logan, was overly curious about the tactical abilities of their fighting vehicles and what they had brought back in the tractor trailer. Marc thought he recognized the early 20s man but when Marc questioned him on it, the man insisted they had never met. The male had brought coffee with him, as a good will gesture. When Marc and Milan turned it down and told him to leave, the man offered up some bourbon. Whereupon, Marc told the man that if he didn't immediately leave, he would be detained for suspicion of being a spy.

Logan went to see Jessica about what he had brought back. Jessica was a bit miffed that he couldn't have at least told her what he was up to. It was clear to Logan that she was irritated with him for not trusting her, and using Walton as "his own personal base of operations, coming and going as he pleased, and showing little concern for those who were desperately trying to stay alive."

Logan on the other hand had heard enough out of her. It was time to set her straight.

"Now you listen to me. I know you are angry with me, and rightfully so. But what you're saying isn't true."

"Yeah, then what did you come back for?" she asked.

Logan needed to make things right, to tell her how he felt. He wasn't a wordsmith when it came to talking to a woman. In fact, he had damn little interaction with any female outside of the military. He told her plainly, hoping the truth would set things right between them.

Candidly, he began, "I still remember the day I left, but I didn't realize what I was leaving behind. Not until the day Benny and I were in our first battle. The Battle of Chambersburg. There were buildings on fire, explosions all around us, soldiers being cut down like summer wheat in a hailstorm, the dying sounds of soldiers from both sides calling out in agony.

We fought and we pushed forward, then fell back, regrouped, and pushed forward again twice more. In the end the UTA withdrew. But what did we get? Bodies. Bodies everywhere—just kids, kids like me. I was ankle deep in corpses. Standing in the middle of the battlefield, screaming at the top of my lungs, "Fuck you, fuck you." Benny. He tries dragging me back from the frontline. But I didn't give a shit. Right there, right then I knew what I had lost. I didn't want to be part of some army, fight in some war, living in some filthy camp. I just wanted to be home, to sleep in my own bed, finish school, see your smile when you sucked on a Teardrop. I no longer had that choice. I was a soldier now. So, I became the best soldier I could be. Fought to stay alive."

Hearing Logan's confession, Jessica's anger was softened. She quietly asked, "So, why did you come back?"

"Because of you..." he revealed. "We've seen a lot of people out there just trying to survive. And we've seen a lot of bad people out there, too, preying on the weak, doing them harm, killing, stealing, and worse. Here you are, taking charge, trying to help others, trying to do some good in the world."

"Yeah, well, I don't think that's going to matter once the Scavs come back."

"If it's the one thing I've learned over these past years, a leader needs a team, needs support to win. We could be that additional support."

"You would do that? You would help me? Even after all I said?"

"Yeah, I would. My team would. We're staying here, going to come up with a plan to defend the town, to make sure the Scavs never hurt another survivor anywhere. That's why we came for Chief Crncevic and the other truck. The Chief was the only one who knew how to drive the tractor trailer. We brought back some supplies—food and weapons."

"You did?"

"Yeah, we did. But don't tell anyone. I really think you have a spy amongst you. If I'm right, the Scavs will be coming real soon. That's why I'd like you to call a meeting with your security team tonight. Then we can discuss my ideas and concerns, and come up with a couple of options on defending your home. You tell me where and what time and I'll bring Benny, Chief Crncevic, and Lt Leger with me. In the meantime, as soon as it's dark, I'd like to get the rifles and ammo we brought back into your armory. If that's okay with you?"

With the weapons loaded into the armory, a thorough discussion between the team on defensive and offensive options, and the meeting with Jessica's people not until midnight, Logan and his team decided to spend a few hours relaxing.

Marc had built a good-sized campfire near the Puma and he along with Logan and Milan were gathered around enjoying one another's camaraderie. Logan decided a little music was required. He got out his Gibson acoustic guitar and harmonica that he brought from home. He started off by performing a Ron Hawkins song that Hawkins had written for his band Lowest of the Low, just as Benny and Kristen strolled into camp arm-in-arm. Since Benny had brought his violin with him, too, Logan urged Benny to retrieve it and join him. As Benny was in the truck tuning his instrument, Logan started his second song which was the first song he had learned to play for his own band. It was Kris Kristofferson's "Me and Bobby McGee." The song had been one of his Uncle Sheridan's favorites, as performed by Janis Joplin. The Bruce Lees performed it like The Highwaymen used to perform it live. However, Logan had a fondness for Kristofferson's stripped-down version recorded on the album *The Austin Sessions*. When Logan got halfway through the tune, Benny joined in with his violin, and then added a backing vocal on the refrain. The two of them followed with "Acadian Driftwood" by The Band. They took turns singing alternate stanzas. Logan transposed the keyboard parts to harmonica. After a minute or two, Marc Romano decided to add a little drumming by tapping on an empty equipment box he was using as a seat. They followed with The Band's song "The Weight." This time Marc got to sing one of the parts and share in the three-part harmony. Marc wasn't the best singer but it didn't matter. They were glad to have him join in.

It didn't take long for Jessica to hear the music drift into her den. She heard Logan's melodic voice. She hadn't heard him sing and play for a very long time. When Jessica heard "The Weight" she decided to go investigate. By the time she approached them, Benny and Logan were playing Merle Haggard's "I'm a Lonesome Fugitive." Kristen saw her cautiously approaching, and she gestured to Jessica to join them. She sat next to Kristen across from Logan and Benny. Blaze moved from Logan's feet to Jessica. She gave him an ample rubbing before Blaze settled at her feet.

Logan smiled at her as he sang. He was happy to see her. When the song was done, he told Benny he hoped he'd remember the next non-band song they had worked on. Logan picked the first half dozen notes on his guitar. Benny remembered immediately. The two of them had spent three days learning the song, Benny having transposed the cello parts into violin. It was OneRepublic's "Apologize."

Jessica was slightly teary-eyed from the song. Kristen nudged Jessica out of her seat and toward Logan. Benny noticed and got up to exchange seats. Jessica tentatively sat down next to him, Blaze following. Logan wiped a tear from her eye. Jessica in turn gave him a huge hug and lip kiss on the lips. Of course, the team, encouraged by Benny, had to applaud. Both Jessica and Logan were slightly embarrassed.

"Are you all done now?" Logan asked. They weren't. "Well, I think it's Benny's turn to sing something to Lieutenant Leger. And being that she's from Jersey, I know the perfect song and so does Benny," Logan announced, as he put his capo onto the neck of his guitar. He continued, "A song written by Bruce Springsteen, but performed ala Mumford & Sons, The Band, but very much in the style the Bruce Lees. Right, Benny?"

Benny tried to wriggle out of it, but his comrades weren't going to have it. Milan began to chant, "Do it, do it, do it!" The others joined in.

Benny acquiesced. "Okay, okay. I never did the lead on this one. It was sung by Katzby, the main singer of the band Logan and I were in."

Kristen didn't tear up during the song, but she did have a wide grin of pleasure and amazement as Benny sang and played "Atlantic City" for her. Plus, there was a very big kiss for Benny at the end of the song, which garnered much attention from the rest of the group, making Benny feel self-conscious. Logan had gotten his payback.

PART V

LIVING WITH WAR

LOGAN KNEW ALL OF JESSICA'S SECURITY PERSONNEL. THERE WAS OF course Katie Troy and Donna Testa but also Barb Schwartz. With exception to Jessica, they were all in the same graduating class. That was if Logan had actually graduated with them.

The women were heavily armed, each with weapons that suited their needs and skills. Katie had a Mossberg 590A3 Tactical shotgun and Glock 22 Gen5 pistol in .40 S&W. Both had been her father's police service weapons. Donna carried a Smith & Wesson M&P 15 Sport III AR-15 with loads of extra magazines. Plus, from what Logan could tell by the manufacturing logo imprinted into the Fingerprint Checkered Wood Grips that protruded from her hip holster, she had an old Colt Wiley Clapp Government 1911 pistol in .45 ACP. He didn't remember her having any special firearms skills, but she had been on the school's archery team. Logan recalled she had won a few regional and territorial championships. Barb Schwartz, Logan remembered had been in the high school's competition rifle and pistol shooting clubs. She still had her MasterPiece Arms Bolt Action Precision Match Rifle (PMR) in .308 Winchester, along with her Smith & Wesson M&P 9mm pistol with a red dot optic sight. Barb had won a number of school competitions as well as two junior regional competitions. Her marksmanship skills were far greater than Logan's in both rifle and pistol. Jessica had her father's Glock 26 pistol with high-capacity magazine and his Daniel Defense DD5 V5 Hunter hunting rifle chambered in .308 Winchester with a 20-round magazine. It was an older model rifle but Logan remembered Henry had told him it had never failed when hunting deer.

Logan was very impressed with the four of them. They were extremely smart and all had sound input into the discussions. Their strengths, smarts, positive attitudes, and firepower made him think of Norse Valkyries, though he didn't think it aloud.

Defensively the safe zone was in better shape than when Logan had left. In his absence, Milan had already barricaded off most of the southern street access from vehicle and foot traffic by using as many school busses, trucks, and vans as they could find. He had constructed a long vehicle wall along the safe zone's southern border, but there were many gaps that had to be filled in with cars. They would also need to add another couple of watchtowers along the vehicle wall.

Earlier in the day Milan and Logan had walked all along Milan's defensive wall, the bridge, the river, both to the East and West, and everything outside the original safe zone doing a survey. Logan used the drone to augment their inspection, during which Milan drew a map and noted the areas with the weakest defensive points. Amongst their discoveries, Logan and Milan realized that there was no easy way to get across the river if the bridge was impassable. There were low points a distance away where their vehicles could ford, but no shallow areas nearby that warfighters could quickly cross. This had to be remedied immediately. Milan and Logan went about as covertly as possible correcting the problem by running a guy rope along the bridge above the waterline. Logan would later, in their meeting with Jessica and her security heads, tell them what they had fashioned.

Logan and Milan presented their proposal on what needed to be done to tighten up their East and West perimeters, along with one particular area of the river that separated the northern portion of the fairgrounds and the southern portion of the canning factory. The water at that section was about two feet deep and could easily be crossed with vehicles with high wheelbases. Plus, there was a grassy area that led to a large gap in the tree line on their side of the river. The enemy could easily ford the water, cut through the fairground, and use Stockton Avenue to make a western advance on the armory and bridge, as another force came across the bridge. Options were limited, since resources were in short supply even with scavenging materials from the other side of the bridge. It would take time and everyone who was capable would need to pitch in so they could get it done quickly. Everyone in the room knew time was not with them.

With the defensive and offensive strategies concluded, Logan moved onto the next topic. It wasn't one he wanted to discuss but it necessary.

"Sad truth is people are going to get hurt, some possibly killed." He told them. "Lieutenant Leger's a surgeon. She'll need a place to operate. And she'll need surgical supplies. Milan tells me the hospital still stands."

Barb Schwartz spoke up, "Hospital was abandoned after the last wave of the virus. It's got a lot of surgical supplies, but not much of anything else."

"Then with Jessica's permission, I'd like to have you show the lieutenant the hospital in the morning. And maybe get one or two people to help out and prep a surgical room."

Logan looked at Jessica for her approval.

"Absolutely," Jessica confirmed. "My mom can help on that. She was a nurse if you recall. Is 7:00 a.m. okay?"

When the meeting was over, Jessica said she would find them all housing accommodations in whatever variation they wanted. She was sure most of them hadn't slept in a real bed for a long time. She even offered them some rooms in her house. Milan had already been staying there. Benny said he'd like his own place for he and Kristen. Logan said he and Marc could stay in a place together, preferably as close to the armory as possible because the four of them were going to take turns guarding the armored vehicles and the Two Guys truck.

Two days later, just after 8:00 a.m., a large contingent of motorcycles and trucks came across the bridge and stopped about 25-yards from the school bus blockade. The occupants of the convoy exited their vehicles armed with automatic rifles but did not initiate an attack. A young man stepped out of the lead vehicle and moved toward the busses. Donna Testa was in the lookout hut that had been newly built on top of the left bus around its roof hatch. It was a wood framed structure with textured steel floor plates on three sides and a wooden roof. Milan had built it along with reinforcing the river facing sides of the busses. When she saw the young man, Donna immediately recognized him. Not only had he been a former classmate of hers, but he was also the one that had previously come looking for Jessica. Donna immediately radioed for her.

"Jessica Miranda!" through a bullhorn the man shouted at the busses. "Time for you to give yourself up, or it's gonna be scorched earth. You got two minutes!"

Logan was in the armory with Jessica, Barb Schwartz, and Katie Troy. He was showing them how to operate a AT6 launcher. When the call from Donna Testa came in, Logan was ready to take command of the situation but he wasn't about to overstep his authority. He asked Jessica first, and told her they could execute the contingency strategy, which was now in place. It was the one in regard to the bridge being impassable if their defensive countermeasures weren't completed prior to the Scavs arrival.

Looking at his watch, the man announced, "Times up. So, what's it going to be?"

Donna shouted back, "Your answer is on the way. Just another minute," she told him, and then disappeared into the bus.

The man called back, "Are you purposely trying to piss me off, or do you genuinely think we'll not kill everyone inside? It's punishment time!"

Logan rose out of the hatch and into the lookout hut with only his Peacemaker revolver strapped to his hip for a weapon, and announced, "She's not home."

The man looked up at Logan and exclaimed, "Well, shit. Everybody hold your fire, it's Logan Ross, the war hero. I heard you came back."

"Holy stink pickle, it's David Katzby!" Logan replied with genuine surprise. "Did your little band of butt monkeys miss the turn off to Sturgis?" he rudely remarked, and then needled David with another crass quip. "You need to turn around and go up the Fudge Freeway... No? Doesn't ring a bell?"

If it had been anyone else that had come demanding Jessica's surrender, Logan would have never pitched his insults. But it was Katzby his former bandmate, and why he was involved with the marauders confounded Logan.

Katzby didn't react to Logan's sarcastic comments. Instead, he got right to business.

"Jessica's not home, huh? Well, I got some news for you. I know that's a lie. Now you're going to give me what I want or there'll be hell to pay."

"There are families in here," Logan reminded him. "There are children and the elderly in here. People that you know are in here."

"And that's exactly why I'm giving Jessica the opportunity to give herself up, along with all the food in the granary and all the weapons in the armory. Oh, yeah, and while we're at it, we'll take the Two Guys truck with us, too. You can have Benny drive it out to me." David told him.

"Oh, I don't think so." Logan returned.

David reminded him, "I got 30 people with guns with me. What do you got? A few girls, some old people, and a few bolt-action rifles."

"Your people have guns; my people have guns. They might be aiming those rifles at you right now. Eyes to sights, fingers to triggers. Bang, bang. Shoot, shoot!"

"Last chance, Logan. Give us what we want or—"

Logan needed to stall longer to allow time for the rear attack team to get across the river and into position. It was not going to be easy for them. The water was cold, it was hip deep, and the current was strong. He also needed a moment more to assess the threat and see if he could get a sense of who was truly in charge of the marauder force. He certainly knew it wasn't Katzby, not the way the Scavs operated. He also saw that some of the automatic rifles they were armed with appeared to be Colt assault rifles and not Sig Sauer or another producer. Colt UTA had been seized and forced out of business nearly twenty years earlier by the UTA government, after Canada invaded and annexed the Alaska Territory for their own. The dissolution had been punishment because Colt Canada was the main firearms supplier to the Canadian military. Logan found it suspicious that many of the weapons were in the same place all at once.

"—Yeah, yeah yeah. You're gonna shoot unless Jessica Miranda surrenders. What do you want with her anyway—? You know what, who gives a shit biscuit. My question is, how did you become such an assclown? I mean, I know you were bitter about changing the band name from The Great Katzbys to The Bruce Lees, but *seriously?*"

"You're all class, Logan... Low."

"As your friend, I'm giving you a chance," Logan told Katzby. "If you don't pull on me, when I start killing everyone around you, you're going to have a choice to make. You can keep choosing this life, and die, or you can figure out someone else to be and live."

Katzby replied, "You got some balls on you, war hero."

An intense looking man in his mid-30s standing four feet behind Katzby whispered something. Logan caught a glimpse of what was clutched in his hand.

"Goodbye, Logan," Katzby said, and then turned as the man behind him raised an Eagle 40mm Grenade Launcher.

Logan pulled his revolver and opened fire, grievously wounding Katzby's whispering man, just as the man pulled the trigger. The grenade rocketed over the busses and then narrowly missed the roof of the grange building as it streaked through the air and exploded somewhere behind the grange. Logan was also able to kill two other enemy combatants before any of them could exchange gunfire. Logan's opening salvo was the signal for everyone to go weapons hot. From the busses, a rifle popped out of every second window and began to discharge.

Jessica, Benny, Marc, Milan, Barb, and Katie had not made it across the river and onto the bridge when the shooting began. The water was cold and the crossing was slow. It took them a few more minutes but when they emerged the enemy was caught completely off guard. Benny, Marc and Milan started their attack with a salvo of hand grenades. Then everyone opened fire as they pushed forward.

When the enemy's return fire began, Logan immediately hit the deck to get out of the line of fire, which was not only directed at him but also at everyone inside the busses. He yelled down to Donna Testa for his MCX Spear assault rifle.

David Katzby and his crew had underestimated Jessica's tenacity, determination, and resources. He was certainly not expecting a rear assault and getting boxed in by a bunch of girls with rifles, even with

Logan's help. After all, the survivors at Walton were up against 30 combatants, many of which were trained soldiers.

The skirmish lasted eight minutes. Some of the enemy tried to flee. As they did, they were cut down. None of those Logan believed to be soldiers made an attempt to surrender. They fought until the last warfighter fell. Thirty enemy combatants lay dead on the bridge—not number 31; David Katzby. He had not pulled any weapon and was hiding behind his pickup truck. When the bullets stopped flying, he raised his hands and surrendered.

Marc, Milan, Benny, Barb, Katie, and Jessica surrounded him. Logan came out to meet them.

"Everyone, okay? he asked. They all were. "Good. Only one injury in the bus. Just a flesh wound from a ricochet," Logan reported. He looked to where the whispering man had fallen but the only traces that remained were the discharged grenade launcher and a blood trail. Logan looked to the frightened Katzby and told his companions. "If he so much as farts, kill him."

Logan walked out onto the bridge and into the death and destruction. He picked up a dropped automatic rifle, and then ventured further out and found the whispering man. Logan pulled his pistol and shot a body on the ground. He returned to Katzby.

Katzby feared for his life. "Don't kill me," he begged. "I didn't pull any weapon."

Logan held up the retrieved assault weapon and declared, "The stamp on this rifle states it's a Colt D6A2 manufactured in Canada. I counted at least eight." Pointing to the ground, Logan added, "Then there's that Eagle II grenade launcher—another Canadian weapon—tells me these aren't just ordinary marauders... You better start singing or I'll do things to you that will make me ashamed to look into a mirror afterward."

To give him motivation to be forthcoming, Logan pointed the Colt rifle to his groin and asked again, "Whose assclown are you?"

Katzby put up his hands and gestured for Logan not to shoot, as he said, "Okay, okay. All I know is they're some sort of elite Canadian

Special Forces unit under the command of a captain named Armitage. They call themselves Lancers."

"And how did you get involved? You're sure the hell not Canadian."

"When they invaded Delhi, my sister and I tried to escape. But they caught us outside—"

There was a sound of a motorcycle starting, Logan looked toward mid-crossing. An enemy combatant was attempting to make an escape. As the motorcyclist hightailed it, Logan jumped up on Katzby's pickup truck and stood on its roof. Benny jumped up on another truck and immediately started shooting. Logan placed the Colt's select fire switch to semi-automatic and took careful aim and the fleeing enemy. Whereas Benny missed with his barrage, Logan's shot hit the motorcycle's gas tank just as the rider turned at the north end of the bridge. The left side drive 6 speed motor bike exploded, sending the operator flying.

"Damn," Benny exclaimed, "that was the most amazing shot I've ever seen."

Logan replied, "The worst! I was aiming at the rider. Piece of crap rifle." He aimed it back at Katzby as he came off the truck and said, "But I'm sure it's a good enough to blow your nutsack off. Now finish," Logan demanded.

"I don't know much, just what I overheard."

"Well, what are they doing here?"

"Didn't hear," David said, and then offered up, "But it must be important since they took Fort Drum, Port Oswego, and Sackett's Harbor."

"You're lying," Logan told Katzby. "Those are too close to Canada. They would have never dropped bombs there."

"They didn't. Heard they sent Lancers in by land and air as the bombs were falling. They killed everyone and took the bases to use as some sort of staging areas."

"Shit!" Milan exclaimed. "I think those are the main bases for the border wall along the St. Lawrence."

"Then what the hell do the Canadians want this far south? Delhi and Walton aren't strategic by any means."

"Don't know."

"So, why are they after me?" Jessica demanded to know.

"Don't know that either. Just that you've been marked a high value target."

"You don't know a lot, do you?" Logan asserted. "But you certainly followed orders."

Katzby returned, "I didn't have a choice. They have my sister. Some of those people you just killed weren't soldiers. They were like me. Forced to do what they said or they'd kill our families."

"One last question," Logan said, and asked, "Who's the spy and how is he/she communicating with you?"

"I don't know who he/she is. All the messages go through the base's communication center."

Logan raised the Colt rifle up to Katzby's chest.

Katzby began to panic. "You said you wouldn't kill me," he nervously reminded Logan.

Logan lowered the rifle and stated, "Oh, I'm not going to kill you, Katzby. But I will—" Logan pulled his holstered Peacemaker and shot Katzby in his left triceps, tearing his flesh.

"What the fuck, Logan!" Katzby cried out in agony, grabbing his wound. "I didn't draw on you."

Observing the wound, Logan told him, "That's not too bad. Armitage sent 30 men with you to Walton. One man returns, a man with no military background, without a scratch. Uh-uh. Your captain won't be an idiot. You return and show him that little scratch; he may just believe you. And don't forget... You still need to figure out someone else to be."

"He's a she. And you can't send me back now. They'll kill me. They'll kill my sister if I go back. I failed."

"Then like I said, you should go figure out someone else to be and live."

"No, no. Kill me. You have to kill me," Katzby pleaded. "If I walk away, they'll know. The spy will see to it. He's probably already radioing them. Please, Logan. Don't let them kill my sister."

Logan didn't argue against it, he simply told Katzby, "Fair enough," and then pointed toward mid-bridge. "Get moving."

The others began arguing that it wasn't right to execute Katzby, not under the extenuating circumstances. Their pleas fell on deaf ears.

Logan turned to Benny and said, "He's going to get exactly what Billy Lo did in *Game of Death*. It's all I can do for him."

It took Benny a moment to understand Logan's reference. He told the others to stand down. It was for the best.

At mid-bridge Logan forced Katzby to his knees. Logan whispered something into his ear before stepping back and pulling the trigger of his revolver. When it was done, Logan picked up Katzby's limp body and tossed him over the bridge rail and down into the river.

Every enemy weapon and ammunition cartridge they could find was foraged, and every corpse disposed of. Afterward, the abandoned vehicles would be repositioned into an obstacle course for the purpose of making the expanse a slow crossing. On the corpse of the whispering man they found a radio. Logan knew it was highly unlikely the radio was being used to communicate with their base, and more likely it was utilized to talk to their spy.

Milan used the Puma's navigation and mapping system to drawn a map of the area in which the Canadians had infiltrated and the known towns they had raided. As the seven of them reviewed the diagram, the tension in the room was intense between Logan and Jessica's people. They were angry over Logan's execution of Katzby and it reflected in all their attitudes. Logan was aware of it but chose to ignore it.

"That pattern," Logan commented. "That looks familiar."

Jessica looked at the pencil sketch and then to Benny. "Perhaps if someone had stayed in school, they'd realize those are all towns and cities along the part of the Erie Canal that connects with the Oswego Canal," she said tersely.

"Of course," Logan said, not looking up from the map. "They could pillage every abandoned city from Oswego to New York and transport the spoils using the canal. Plus, they could effectively annex the New England Colonial Territory and a sizable chunk of the New York District. But why Delhi and Walton? *Just for you?*" Logan looked up to Jessica and continued, "You're of no military significance. No offense."

Jessica hadn't taken any offense to his remark, but the room was still thick with disapproving looks and tension.

Benny had enough. "Okay, Logan. Either you tell them or I will."

"Fine," Logan said. "You tell them."

"Logan didn't kill David," Benny announced.

Jessica rebuked Benny's statement. "We all saw Logan shoot him, then toss him into the river."

"You saw exactly what I wanted you to see," Logan said in a matter-of-fact tone. "Exactly what I needed all of you to see."

"*What?*" Jessica asked.

Logan looked at Benny to expound. Benny explained, "That weird comment Logan made about Billy Lo. That was a reference to a Bruce Lee film. In the movie Billy Lo faked his death."

Looking at Logan, Katie said, "But we all saw you shoot him." The rest were in agreement.

"David could be a bit of a tool at times but he was a friend, a band mate, a brother. If I was going to shoot him, I would have done so facing him," Logan assured them. "If he didn't drown, then he's hope-fully doing what I told him, figuring out someone else to be."

Jessica was a bit miffed at the ruse. "Well, why didn't you tell us what you were going to do?"

"Because. Because I needed everyone—all of you, everyone in the busses—to believe I killed David. I'm sorry I had to deceive every-body but there's a spy in your group. I needed to make sure that spy believed David was dead, so those Canadians won't kill his sister. And now that you know, it needs to stay in this room, for David and his sister's sake."

The spy. Who was the spy? Time was running out. The spy would have reported what had transpired on the bridge and that the soldiers had been defeated. It was a little over three hours from Walton to Fort Drum and less than three if the enemy was coming from Oswego, NY. Fort Drum was also over 160 miles from Walton, so Logan knew that whoever the spy was, they were certainly not using a handheld radio. It had to be a base transceiver, a powerful one with a high antenna to reach the bases.

"Chief Crncevic and his fabrication crew have completed their river defense build, and we need to implement its placement immediately—before the Canadians get here; which I figure is in 90 minutes, max," Logan told the group. "Except the only issue is, if we do so, the spy is certain to find out and relay it to the Canadians. So, this brings us to the spy. We need to find this person immediately."

Jessica asked, "Are you sure they'll be coming. After all, we did just wipe out a bunch of them."

"Oh, I'm sure. With you being public enemy number one and us taking out 30 of them—

they'll come at us with a sizable force on two fronts. Now... A couple of things I heard since I came back don't add up. First, when we ran into Principal Weiss in Delhi, he said that he heard or got the word the Scavs were hitting every town from Jacksonburg to Fulton. Why is it no one got wind that they were coming to Delhi? Who was supplying you the information?"

"The Home Guard," Jessica said.

"Okay, so how were they getting the information?"

Jessica explained, "Through HAM radio. The Home Guard had it set up inside the university radio station."

"The college radio station on Bronco Drive?"

"It was until it burned down," Jessica replied.

"Three days after the Scavs came," Logan said, needing clarification.

"Yes. The same night my house burnt down."

Logan became very suspicious. "Principal Weiss said that Jim Reynolds—Scruffy—was found on Bronco Drive nearly dead. Was there a reason for him to be on campus?" he asked.

"He was part of the Home Guard radio team."

"*Really?* And who else was on the team?"

"My father, he was second in charge. He was supervised by a lieutenant from the Walton Territorial Guard base. Then there was Danny, Katie's brother." Katie nodded her head in agreement. "Also, Paul Roth the postmaster. But he was killed when the Scavs raided Delhi. Then Gino Mando—no. Gino Mado, Madanello. Gino Madanello."

"You said, 'Mando'."

"Sorry," Jessica apologized. "Sometimes I stumble on his name."

Logan turned to Benny and said, "She said 'Mando.' Jim said 'Go mando. Hurt, hurt, bang, bang.' Right?"

"Mando," Benny repeated. "That's what Scruffy said."

Logan pounded a fist on Jessica's desk, and semi-cursed, "son-of-a—!"

"What's that about?" Jessica asked.

Logan explained, "Jim got upset when we were discussing his assault. It was just gibberish, Principal Weiss said, because of his brain injury. But now it makes sense. Eliminating the lieutenant and Bob Roth, that leaves three people. Your dad. Salt of the Earth. Not the kind of man that would betray his family or his country. That leaves Danny and Gino."

"Can't be my brother," Katie interjected. "He's got nothing against Jessica; they weren't even classmates. Didn't really know one another. Right?" Katie asked Jessica for substantiation.

Jessica confirmed, "No way, not Danny. He's proved he's trustworthy."

"And Danny has been on my fabrication crew," Milan added. "Good kid, hard worker. Smart, too."

"That leaves Gino," Logan announced. "Which might explain why you didn't know about Buffalo or that Walton was going to be attacked. Where's the radio setup?"

"We don't have a radio anymore," she told him. "The Scavs destroyed the police station where it was."

"If someone is communicating with the Canadian military, then there has to be a radio. And there would have to be a high antenna, like the one at the Territorial Guard Base."

"Stripped," Barb said. "The building is completely emptied and checked four times a day."

"Then the hospital or the fire department."

"No antenna at the hospital and the one at the fire department was destroyed when it burnt down," Barb said.

"Any other location that any of you can think of with a high antenna?"

"I think the oldies station out on Radio Station Road is still there," Donna remarked.

Logan knew exactly what Donna had commented on. "You're right, the oldies station. Sophomore year class trip for career days."

Milan acknowledged. "That'll work. All you have to do is mount an all band antenna on top of it with a long cable run. Then hook up your transceiver."

"Why are you certain it's Gino?" Katie asked. "What would be his motivation? He lived in Delhi like the rest of us."

Logan looked at his watch. "We're cutting it close. We have to deploy the troops and set the defenses, one way or the other." Logan turned to Katie. "I don't know for sure. The National Guard lieutenant or another someone could have been a Canadian plant. Is there anyone else in your group that raises suspicion?" he asked, looking at Jessica. "Anyone come with you that wasn't from Delhi or showed up to Delhi or Walton before the Scavs came?"

All of Jessica's people took a moment to think but couldn't come up with anyone that met the criteria.

Jessica commented, "It couldn't have been the lieutenant; the guard base closed before Delhi was raided. The only one who came to Walton after Delhi got hit and before Walton was first invaded was Gino. But that's only because—" Jessica covered her mouth as she gasped. "Holy shit biscuits. Gino went north with about 150 Delhi survivors. He was the one who insisted it was safe where they were going. A couple of days later he arrived in Walton and joined the Home Guard radio team. I didn't hear it first-hand, but rumor had it that the

Delhi survivors were attacked before they got to Lake Placid. Only a few escaped, Gino being one of them."

"Has anyone seen him this morning?"

"He was on the body removal team earlier," Katie confirmed. "But they finished a half hour ago. I can send someone to his residence to see if he's there."

Madanello wasn't home, so Jessica ordered an all-out search for him. Logan had his suspicion that Madanello had gone to report what had happened. It had been 90-minutes since the Canadians' defeat. If Madanello hadn't reported what had happened by now, Logan was certain that the Canadian strike team's failure to report in would raise an alarm with their base.

Most of the survivors had gathered in the parking lot of the armory as requested by Jessica. If a heavily armed military force was looming, she needed to make sure the very young and elderly were safe. She was going to send them eight miles away to a secluded and abandoned restaurant. Only those assigned to the escort detail knew where the small group would be headed. However, Jessica was greeted with dissension and anger toward her. When someone yelled out, "Why should we listen to a teenage girl," Logan had heard enough disrespect. His temper flared. He grabbed his Peacemaker revolver and shot it into the air. The unruly mob immediately went silent.

"You ungrateful whiners," Logan scolded them. "Who in the hell do you think you are? If it wasn't for Jessica most of you would have been dead already."

"Says who?" an angry female voice rang out.

"Let me remind you what happened the last time someone didn't listen to Jessica, as in your town mayor and the Home Guard. They laughed at her observations and warnings about poor defensive preparations, did they not? And what happened then?" Logan asked. No one responded. "Oh, you've all forgotten? Didn't the town fall to the Scavs, and didn't Jessica save all of you Waltoners by gathering you inside the safety of the armory? Hasn't she and her team kept you safe, healthy, and fed since then?" he pointed out.

Logan's words fell mostly on deaf ears. A mid-40s woman told Logan, "They don't care about us; they want her," she pointed at Jessica. "Give the Scavs what they want and they'll leave us be."

"These aren't scavengers," Logan enlightened those gathered. "They're Canadian military." Logan looked over the crowd. "I don't know why they are hell-bent after Jessica, but they won't be satisfied with just her. You've seen what they've previously done. What makes you think it will be any different?"

There was a grumble followed by more dissension. A short Asian woman in her late 50s with long black hair shouted out, "Then we should leave, go further south. Why should we risk our lives for her or this place?"

The group began to agree with the rebellious woman. Jessica tried to convince them that staying and fighting for their home was what should be done, but they refused to listen. When the crowd grew surly and threatened Jessica's well-being, Logan shot his pistol into the air for a second time.

"You really think it'll be safe anywhere if the Canadian military decides that the entirety of America is to be annexed?" Logan asked them. "You think they're going to give a damn about some Americans? Or have you forgotten about the bombs that wiped out our country? There might not be much left of America but I'm damn well going to defend what remains, and so are all of you."

"We don't have to listen to you. You're nothing but a kid, too," the Asian woman said with defiance. The majority of the riled-up crowd agreed with her.

"Yeah, I'm a kid," Logan admitted, and then added, "A kid whose seen four years of bloody conflict, only to come home to find out my town was razed by Canadians pretending to be scavengers. I won't let that happen here again. Not after you've all worked so hard at building a home and future here."

The woman was even more rebellious, with most of the survivors backing her. "You have no stake in this town and we certainly don't have to listen to you." She turned to those closest to her and stated, "I'm leaving and so should all of you. To hell with this place."

"What's your name," Logan asked her.

The woman was leery. "Why? What's it to you?"

"I just wanted to know the name of the person that seems to be speaking for everyone."

"Missy. Missy Trechak," she said.

"Well, *Missy*. I just want you to know if any of these fine folks attempts to leave, I'll shoot you first," Logan notified her.

Some of the crowd gasped, hearing Logan's brash statement.

"*What!?*" Missy exclaimed with shock and anger at Logan's announcement.

Logan replied, "I will shoot you in the legs, tie you to a chair, and strap a rifle in your arms if necessary. But you will not run, you will fight." Logan then addressed the crowd. "Any of you. And I mean *any* of you try and hightail it out of here," he warned, "I will have my soldiers shoot you as deserters. None of you are running. You will help defend this sanctuary, and I swear to God that if any of you do manage to getaway, when it's all over, I will hunt you down and butcher you like a pig," he said with a cold, hard look. "Now get the elderly and youngsters together so we can get them to safety, and see Jessica and her team for your duty assignments. Now move!" Logan ordered.

With Logan's threat, there was no more opposition, even from the main protagonist Missy Trechak. As the crowd dispersed, Benny turned to Logan and said, "That was a hell of a motivational speech. Thought you were going to shoot that woman just to make your point."

"Sometimes what is needed is a good herd dog to keep the flock from going astray," Logan said.

Benny returned, "Sounded more like a Southern Baptist preacher putting the fear of God into the flock."

PART VI

PEACE OF MIND

TIME WAS OF THE ESSENCE TO PREPARE FOR ANOTHER IMMINENT attack. Logan wasn't sure if they were coming again in trucks and on motorcycles or would show up in fighting vehicles. He was certain, though, that they wouldn't be sending more forced civilians into action. The next strike would be coming from highly skilled soldiers and they would certainly be heavily armed. He also knew the enemy wasn't going to give Jessica the courtesy of surrendering like Katzby had done. The bus blockade was not going to be a deterrent and Logan feared that anyone inside—steel plate enforced or not—was at a high risk of being killed. Logan advised Jessica not to post gunners inside the busses but behind the secondary barricade of vehicles that lined the front of the granary and armory.

As Milan and his team set out their booby traps, Benny moved the HGC into position. There was a house off of More Avenue with a long driveway. To the tree lined rear of the house was the eastern edge of the fairgrounds. To the North was the river. If the Canadians broke through the defenses that Milan was setting up—in the water, along the river's edge—the Canadians would use More Avenue as their approach to the armory and bridge.

As for the Puma, Logan intended to use it for a rear attack on the bridge invasion force. They still had a large amount of ammunition for the Patriot gun, plus they still had five AT6 rocket launchers, which had been dispersed amongst the troop leaders. Logan just needed to position the Puma in a place where it wouldn't be seen by the invading force, but close enough to quickly get to the bridge. Jessica told him there was a road called High Street. It was off of Delaware Street that ran parallel with the West Branch Delaware River. High Street was the farthest street east on the northern side of the river of Walton proper and only four blocks from the bridge. Logan did a reconnaissance and a feasibility assessment of the street. It was a bit too far from the bridge and from the main road to the bridge. The enemy would see their approach. Logan chose a different location, the Barstow Feed & Seed store on Delaware Street near North Street. There he could park the Puma inside the attached garage, and then use the narrow pathway along the backs of a couple of businesses that skirted the river. It would put the Puma at the bridge crossing in under 90 seconds.

For hours, everyone awaited the Canadians' arrival. Five hours after the projected time, Logan radioed Jessica and her team that the Puma was returning to the south side of the bridge. If the Canadians hadn't immediately come for a retaliatory strike, Logan was certain there must have been a reason. To what extent the delay was, was something Logan hoped to discover. The only way to possibly find out the Canadians' agenda was to find the one person that might feasibly know—Gino Madanello.

———

Shortly after being dismissed from the body removal detail, Gino Madanello faked he was heading home. Instead, he zig-zagged between some unoccupied houses, cut across a few streets, and then traversed the river's edge where he used the tree line as camouflage, avoiding the security patrols and sentry stations. Once away from the safe zone, he retrieved a hidden bicycle and hastily made his way down NY-206 toward the radio station. The entire three-and-a-half-mile foot and bicycle trip could have been done in under 60 minutes, but Madanello was in a hurry to report the Canadians' devastating defeat to their base. Rushing along the road's shoulder, Madanello disrupted a family of boars feeding along the highway's grassy edge. A massive, angry and aggressive female boar charged at him in protection of its shoats. Sharply swerving to avoid being gored by the unusually large animal, Madanello hit a deep pot hole. The bicycle came to an abrupt halt when the front wheel slammed into the hole's outer edge causing the tire to blow out and the wheel to twist. The force of the sudden impact pitched Madanello over the handlebars and nearly 8 feet through the air, before he came crashing down on his right shoulder, dislocating it. Violently tumbling repeatedly on the hard grit laden asphalt, he struck his head before coming to a rest another eight feet from where he landed. Unconscious and with bleeding cuts, Madanello laid on the pavement for over an hour before awakening. Battered, bruised, and still bleeding, he limped his way down the state thorough-fare with a painful left ankle, a gashed elbow, and a displaced shoulder, still determined to make it to the radio station.

His agonizing journey was marked by a constant need to stop and rest every 400-500 yards. However, he refused to let his excruciating injuries dissuade him. He hobbled into the woods to find a branch to use as a crutch, and a tree to slam his shoulder into to force it back into place. What should have been less than an hour journey to the trans-ceiver station took him nearly three hours.

Logan knelt down and examined the damaged bicycle. He looked at the disheveled gravel and scuff marks. The telltale signs of the bike wreck appeared to be not more than a day old, especially the blood left behind. A bicyclist on an unused road, heading in the same direction as the radio station was too coincidental to be anyone else but their spy. Perhaps, Madanello had been in a hurry and hadn't been paying attention.

At a brisk walk, Madanello might be able to do the remainder of the trip in 45 minutes. If he had been injured from the accident, then perhaps an hour or more, depending on the severity of his wounds, Logan reckoned. This still left Madanello with plenty of lead time. Even so, the Canadians had ample time to send in a quick reaction force. It was puzzling to Logan why there had been no immediate retaliation.

Marc pulled the Puma off the side of the road about a quarter mile from the radio station turn off. In less than ten minutes from disem-barking they were at the abandoned broadcast station. The front of the building had been boarded up and still remained secured. There were no signs of forced entry. When they got around back, it was a different story. The rear steel exit door had been forced open.

It didn't take long to find Madanello. All the two had to do was follow the sound of the unintelligible voices they heard. The room in which the vocal exchange was happening in was the only room that was lighted, too. Logan and Benny were going to simultaneously toss in stun grenades to disorient Madanello in order to quickly subdue him. However, Logan gave a hand signal to hold. From the ajar door, they could understand the conversation Madanello was having with the person on the other end of the transceiver. The verbal exchange sounded a bit heated. The conversation had to do with Madanello being unhappy about having to wait so long to speak to whomever the female was he was speaking to, especially after having made his report on the raiding party to her subordinate hours earlier. Madanello then made mention that she owed him for all he had done, and then demanded she fulfill her end of the arrangement as promised. He told her they needed to drop bombs on the town or send in drones to blow it up. The woman on the other end was very blunt with Madanello in her response. She first called him an idiot and then asked him if he knew what covert operation meant. She then informed him she didn't give a damn about their arrangement. If he had given her proper intel on the situation in the first place, her soldiers wouldn't have been killed. She had every intention of sending in a strike force to wipe everyone out, but her forces were spread thin with the canal campaign. She said if he was in a hurry to see the leader of his group dead, he should grow some big boy balls and do it himself. The conversation ended with her telling Madanello that an assault force would be sent in two days for a pre-dawn raid. If he was still in town by then, he would be considered a hostile combatant.

Madanello was clearly unhappy with what he had been told. Aggravated he cursed, "Stupid bitch."

Logan and Benny tossed in their stun grenades.

Gino Madanello didn't know exactly what had happened to him at the radio station. There was a loud explosion and a bright white flash that had disoriented him. What had followed and how he came to be tied to what he believed to be a chair, his hands bound behind him, and with something over his head preventing him from seeing was as big of a mystery as was his throbbing head injury. He was certain he knew why he had been subdued and restrained, though.

There was a voice behind him that instructed someone to untie his hands. Then the same voice told him to put his hands on the table in front of him, palms down. When Madanello didn't immediately comply, the voice snapped, "You heard me, bitch. Hands on the table." The directive was followed by a brusque, hard slap to the back of his head and the order of, "*Now!*" This time Madanello did as ordered. Until he could assess his situation and formulate a plan of escape, he thought it best to comply.

His left hand was grabbed and held securely. Madanello let out a howl of excruciating pain. Something had been driven through his flesh. Blindly he went to grab for the pointed instrument to pull it free, but was met with a hard strike to his triceps and a warning of, "*Don't,*" by the same male voice that had told him to lay his hands down.

When the covering was removed from his head, the first thing he saw was a nail protruding from the top of his left hand. The nail had penetrated deeply into the wooden tabletop, pinning him.

"Hello, Coffee Boy," Marc greeted him. Madanello recognized the soldier from the armory parking lot, but this was not the voice of the person from moments earlier.

As Marc moved around to the front of the table, Madanello glanced about the room trying to figure out where he was and what his options were for escape. The only immediate objects he could use were some woodworking tools on the countertop before him. Looking left and right he noticed exits at the far ends of the rectangular space. His first impression had been a storage shed, but the building's wooden structure, its support beams, its partially lit overhead fluorescent lighting, and the two opposite egresses told him otherwise. He was inside one of the exhibition buildings at the Delaware County Fair. An approaching figure from behind cast an elongated shadow onto the table. Someone was now above him. Madanello looked up. A familiar faced glowered at him. It was the face of a very pissed off Logan Ross.

"What the fuck, Logan? What's this all about?" Madanello asked in a painful tone, feigning ignorance to why he was being tortured.

Logan moved to Madanello's right side, and told him, "Civilized people need to follow rules. And I'm here to put things right."

"Civilized!? A civilized person wouldn't nail someone's hand down, especially a soldier of The Republic."

Logan returned, "War has changed me. I've learned to be morally flexible."

"Why am I here? What is this all about?" he demanded to know.

Logan pulled out his tactical knife and plunged it into Madanello's leg. Madanello let out another wail of agonizing pain, much more intense than the last. It reverberated off the wooden walls. With tears running down his cheeks, his cry was followed with a livid but pained, "Shit. Motherfucker!"

"I'm a busy man, my time valuable. Having said that, I feel under the circumstances, I owe it to all the people you've had a hand in murdering, irrevocably injuring, and putting in harm's way to give you my full attention," Logan said, and then clarified his intent. "This is not an exercise in torture, nor is it a life lesson to make you a better person. This is an amalgamation of all the sinful choices you've made coming to an ill-fated end. You must accept the consequences of your actions, no matter how torturous, how painful, or how horrible they may seem."

"Fuck you, Logan," Madanello defiantly spit out.

Sadistically, Logan put a hand on the butt of the knife embedded in Madanello's leg and firmly pressed down. Madanello wailed again. "That's fuck you, First Sergeant Ross," Logan replied in a calm whisper. "Now, I pretty well understand your dealings with the Canadians, including the retaliation strike that's coming. What I don't know is why you're working with them. Aiding and abetting an enemy of our nation is treason. So, tell me."

Still insolent, Madanello once again venomously spat, "Fuck you, asshole."

Logan had no tolerance for Madanello's continued disrespect. He grabbed the man's right wrist and slammed his hand down onto the table. Before Madanello could react, Marc came down on his fingers with a five-inch Beechwood mallet that he had snatched up. The brutal blow destroyed the ends of three fingers. The strike had been too much for Madanello. As he began to scream in agony, his eyes rolled up and he fell unconscious.

Madanello didn't know how long he had been out, but he was awoken by Logan repeatedly shouting his name and tapping him on the shoulder.

"That's right, Gino. Wake up, Gino, wake up!" Logan instructed.

When Madanello came to, he was immediately struck by the horribly severe pain in his right hand. He tried to raise it, but it too was nailed to the table top. Seeing his gruesome, pulverized finger tips, Madanello shook his head with shock and fear, and cried, "No, no, no."

"I told you it was First Sergeant Ross," Logan reminded him. "You still have another seven to go, plus ten toes. Unless you choose to unburden yourself by confessing."

Marc picked up an 8mm straight chisel, and with a wicked grin he mocked, " 'This little piggy went, wee, wee, wee all the way home!' "

"Okay, okay," Madanello pleaded. "I'll tell you. I'll tell you... Payback is a bitch named Jessica Miranda," he said coldly.

"What the stink pickle does that mean?"

Paraphrasing Logan, he told the two of them, "This is an amalgamation of all the hurtful choices the people of Delhi and Jessica Miranda have made coming to a well-deserved end."

Logan looked at Marc and said, "I think you hit him in the head too hard. He's non-sensical."

"You don't get it, do you? It's payback for what Jessica did to me at school."

Logan remembered what Jessica had done to Madanello in the school cafeteria. No one at Delaware Academy Middle/High School could forget that Jessica had put the school bully in his place. "You're not seriously telling me that you betrayed your country, had people slaughtered, because a 13-year-old girl kicked you in your nutsack for being an ass snapper?"

"Nothing was the same after that. She made me the laughing stock of school and the town. I lost my friends. Lost respect. I'd walk down the street and people would point and laugh—and I couldn't get a job after graduation. All because that Miranda bitch came to your rescue."

"You watch your lang—"

"You're an asshole!" a loud voice came from behind him.

Madanello thought he had heard someone gasp behind him after Marc had come down on his fingers with the hammer, and now he was certain of the third person in the room. It was Jessica Miranda.

"I didn't do it for Logan," Jessica clarified as she confronted him. "I did it for all the kids in school who were in constant fear of you. You wouldn't even stop after you got two suspensions. You just beat on people outside of school. So, I decided everyone needed to see who you truly were. A pathetic, weak, and insecure loser who, without his friends backing him up, had no power over anyone."

"You ruined my life!" Madanello pathetically cried.

"And you murdered dozens, out of a misguided, petty vendetta." Jessica hauled off and punched Madanello in the jaw. "That's for my father." She struck him again, this time to his nose. "That's for my house." Another painful punch to Madanello's face followed with an addendum of, "And that's for all those you have killed."

With her last punch, Jessica had missed the side of Madanello's face and instead struck him hard in the eye, hurting her knuckles on his brow ridge. Jessica shook off the discomfort.

Madanello laughed at her, calling her a stupid bitch. Jessica picked up a chisel and slammed it down on his pinned hand, cleanly chopping off a finger. Madanello's first reaction was to pull back his hand. He almost tore it from the nail.

"You fucking cunt!" he screamed at her.

In return for his derogatory remark, she slammed the chisel down again, snipping another digit from his hand. "Go ahead, say it again," she baited him with raised chisel ready to strike again.

"Fuck! Fuck! Fuck!" Madanello cried as he squirmed in pain.

"And what about Jim Reynolds? What did he ever do to you?" Logan asked, as he casually tossed Madanello's detached digits aside. Madanello didn't reply. Logan looked to Marc and said, "Looks like some little piggies need a trim."

"Okay, okay," Madanello conceded. "He had the bad luck of showing up early to his shift, and overheard something he shouldn't have. Wasn't going to let him ruin everything. So, I hit him in the head a few times with the desktop microphone. Then I torched the station. Never figured he'd make it out."

"You shit-swizzling, brainless weathercock. Whining about being laughed at and no one giving you respect. Did it ever occur to you that if you would have reported the Canadian incursion, prevented those other towns from being wiped out, you would have been a hero? No, of course not. Your head's so far up your shit hole you were blind to your own redemption. And now here you are, atoning for your treachery and sins."

Madanello looked up with his bloody, battered, and swollen face, and told Logan, "Doesn't matter what you do to me now. The Canadian's are coming to wipe you all out. I'll have my revenge."

"You sure about that?" Logan asked him. "Then again, you'll never know." Logan picked up the wooden mallet, and before he slammed it into the side of Madanello's head, he told him, "This is for Jim Reynolds."

The hour was nearly 9:00 p.m. There was nothing more they could do at the moment to prep for the coming Canadians. There would be time enough tomorrow to add additional defenses, which Logan had a few ideas for, depending on what resources he could scavenge. For now, sleep was needed for at dawn he, Marc, Milan, and Benny, along with a couple of volunteers, would travel to Delhi to C E Kiff, where they had previously stopped to get diesel fuel. Kiff was an old company founded in the 1880s and one of only three remaining suppliers of heating oil and kerosene, on-road and off-road diesel, gasoline, and propane left in the district.

Most of Logan's team were in their respective homes, trying to unwind, for they all knew it was going to be a long forthcoming forty-eight hours. Marc, however, was in the Puma behind the communications console. He was waiting for the next Republic military communications satellite to come in range. While he waited his thoughts were on his girlfriend he left behind in Delhi. Though Marc knew it was safer for her at the Ross residence, it didn't ease his longing for her any less.

Milan was at the Miranda residence, staying in the guest bedroom on the first floor. He, too, was having difficulty sleeping and found himself in the kitchen with Luci, playing cards and drinking coffee. Very excited, he exclaimed, "Best night ever!" and then displayed his hand and announced, "Gin."

Benny and Kristen knew they weren't going to be able to just get in bed and fall asleep for reasons other than their burgeoning romance and their desire to be intimate with one another. Waiting the day for the Canadian troops to attack had worked them up and they needed to relax before getting any sleep. Luckily, the house they were given had a freestanding, two-person soaking tub. Albeit there was no bubble bath or bath salts to use, but the warm water, a few used candles they had found for ambience, their bathtub spooning, and the bottle of tequila they shared helped to ease their anxiety.

Logan knew he would be lucky if he would get four hours sleep. As team commander it was his duty and moral obligation to go over every detail of the defenses of the upcoming attack, to ensure they were prepared and could keep casualties to a minimum. What bothered him was not having any intel on the firepower and transport vehicles the Canadians would use in their offensive. Would they attack Walton again as they had done twice before, under the guise of being scavengers? Or would they risk bringing heavier armed vehicles with them. The not knowing was what was stressing him. To help relieve his fretfulness, he decided to play some guitar.

When the knock came to his second-floor bedroom door shortly after 10:30 p.m., he thought it was Marc, coming to give him a sitrep on the communications effort. He was surprised to find Jessica and Blaze at the threshold. Jessica hadn't immediately knocked when she had arrived. She heard him playing and singing. Logan had been sitting on a chair in his underwear performing one of the many songs he used to sing to her at the bus stop. The song was called "Infinite," and it was one of Jessica's favorites of Logan's repertoire. The song's music and lyrics had been penned by one of Logan's favorite music artists, Ron Hawkins. Hawkins was Canadian. Canadian music was the only allowed import into the country, with the stipulation it wasn't paid for. The song was released by Hawkins in 2017. Since Hawkins had been dead for many years, his music was considered to be in the American public domain.

Logan was caught off guard by her passionate advance. Jessica grabbed onto him, gave him a very impassioned kiss, and then proceeded to push him backward across the room and onto the bed, where she then presented him with a tattered brown paper bag filled with various condoms.

"Strap one on," she told him. "I'm not going to take any chances and end up dying a virgin."

Logan looked into the bag. He was taken aback. Jessica already had her gun belt and shirt off, and was removing her bra when he said, "No, Jessica. Not like this."

Jessica looked at him. As she hurriedly started unbuckling her pants, she told him, "I don't want any alien popping out of me in nine months—just in case. So, I *really* need you to use one."

Jessica had been in such a hurry to get undressed, she had forgotten to take off her boots. Sitting next to him on the bed, she told him. "Don't wait for me. Take the shirt off and drop the skivvies."

Logan looked at her naked torso. She had beautiful, full, symmetrical breasts on a lean and muscular frame. She was indeed physically desirable. Then again, it wouldn't have mattered to him if she still had the same body she had the day he left for the war—which he also had found physically pleasing.

Her wanting lips gave him another passionate kiss as she pushed him back onto the bed. Jessica reached down and began to fondle his manhood. She commented, "It's so... so soft. Shouldn't you be hard?"

Logan pushed her off and said, "No. No, I can't do this."

It wasn't that he didn't want her. He felt like the only reason she had come to his bed was to lose her virginity. Logan didn't want to just fuck Jessica. He wanted to experience the awkwardness of their sexual exploration of one another—to linger in the tenderness, the passion, and the beauty of their lovemaking—to feel her excited, quivering body as she climaxed, and to hold her lovingly after their physical intimacy.

Yes, he knew it was fantasy, but even if only part of it came to fruition then he would be satisfied. After all, his first sexual dalliance had been more like rudimentary sex-ed than a romantic liaison. Sure, it had been a sexually gratifying and an illuminating experience but far from emotionally fulfilling.

"It's okay. It's probably from the stress and anxiety of what's to come."

"No. That's not it. I don't want to fuck you," he said without thinking of how he impolitely had spurned her.

Jessica's face lit with shock and her voice reflected hurt as she exclaimed, "Oh, my God! You couldn't tell me this before I got undressed and fondled your dick?"

Jessica felt horrified and ashamed for making her blatant sexual advance, and letting herself be emotionally vulnerable and physically naked, believing Logan desired her as much as she did him. Humiliated by his rejection, she called him an "emotionally stunted asshat." Then gathered up her belongings and tried to run out of the room before she began to cry. That was one thing she was not going to do in front of him.

Logan realized he had indeed been an asshat for blurting out his tactless remark, instead of giving a thoughtful reason for turning her down. He felt less of a man for it. He had once told Benny in regard to Kristen's aggressive sexual advances that, "It isn't just about sex. It's about her need for physical intimacy and companionship for the night." Logan cursed "shit" under his breath, realizing he probably had come to a hasty assumption. He rushed to the door and blocked her flight.

"Yeah, I'm an asshat," he confessed. "But I take offense to being called emotionally stunted."

"Logan Ross, get your ass out of my way," she demanded, "or I'll kick you in your limp dick."

"Now you're just being mean and vindictive."

"I mean it," she angrily promised.

"You want out? Then give me 60 seconds to apologize, please?"

"59," she returned, as she began to dress. "58-57..."

"I'm sorry for being insensitive and thinking only of my own emotional needs and not yours, too. By the hurt in your angry voice, I realize it took a lot of courage to allow yourself to be emotionally and physically exposed. I'm truly sorry I dismissed you. But you have to understand, it's not that I don't want you, I *really* do. It's that I always thought if sex between us ever happened, we would decide together and it would mean something. I need it to mean something and not something either of us will regret afterward."

Damn, Logan Ross, Jessica thought. There he goes again with one of his beautiful, honest, and meaningful apologies. She punched him hard in the upper chest.

"Okay, I deserve that," Logan acknowledged.

"You're such an asshat," she told him and then punched him again. This time a little lower.

"Ouch," Logan said, flinching. "That was my tit."

"You're such an asshat," she said again in a less angry tone.

"I think we already established that."

"An asshat for thinking my intention was anything other than—"

Logan grabbed onto her and pulled her close. He gave her the most passionate kiss he had given any woman, considering there had only been one other. At first Jessica was stunned at his impassioned advance, but quickly dropped the remainder of her clothes and succumbed to the moment.

"I'm guessing that's not a pistol in your pants," Jessica slyly remarked.

Logan answered by sweeping her off her feet and into his arms. He carried her to the bed, where he gently set her down, then kissed her once more before he moved to his nearby rucksack.

"Where are you going?"

Logan turned to her as he opened his pack. Smiling he said, "Oh, I just want to prove I'm not a total emotionally stunted asshat."

Logan held up a familiar bag.

Surprised, Jessica said, "Is that—? No way! It can't be."

"Oh, but it is. Now who's emotionally stunted?" he baited, as he crawled into bed.

Eagerly, Jessica held out her hands for the gift.

Logan gestured a hand over, but then snatched the bag away just as it touched Jessica's fingers.

"Aww," she said with a frown. "Not fair."

Logan retrieved a single Teardrop from its packaging, unwrapped its light-blue colored foil and held it with his index finger and thumb and told her, "Lips. Bring those beautiful lips right here," he gestured with the chocolate. When she moved within inches, he instructed, "Close your eyes."

With closed eyes Logan rubbed the quick melting chocolate on her lips as if applying a coat of lip gloss. "Now taste," he said.

As Jessica rolled her tongue around her lips, Logan put the chocolate in his mouth and then gave her a kiss, pushing the chocolate into hers. Jessica moaned passionately, "Oh, my God. These are so much better than I remember." The erotic exchange began to make her moist. Jessica put her forehead against Logan's and then kissed him. She apologized, "I'm sorry I called you emotionally stunted," and with a mischievous smile told him, "but we'll have to work on the asshat part." She put her hands around his neck and kissed him again.

Logan responded with another tease. He put another piece of the soft-bite chocolate to her lips and then quickly put it in his mouth. She gave him a sigh and a look of displeasure. Logan retrieved the melting Teardrop and then swirled it around one of Jessica's areolas and over her nipple.

"*Logan!*" she exclaimed with surprise but not objection.

He repeated the chocolate coating on her other breast, and then gently lowered her to the bed. He followed by unwrapping two more Teardrops, one for Jessica to suck on and the other for his enjoyment. This time Logan used it to draw an arrow pointing to Jessica's navel, and then deposited the leftover in her bellybutton for later retrieval.

He moved back to her and began a series of sensual kisses that went from her lips, to her ear lobes, down her neck, and to her left breast, then to the other. He lovingly teased each nipple by slowing licking and sucking each one clean of the confectionary residue. When done, he followed the arrow he had drawn to her bellybutton, sucked the chocolate out, and then continued down, pulling off her panties.

Logan kissed and licked the inside of her inner thighs and her shaved mound. The sensation was nearly as arousing as when he had stimulated her sensitive nipples and made them erect. When his tongue began to probe her vagina, she moaned from the thrill of the new sensation. His wet, warm attentive tongue felt so pleasurable as it moved about.

Then Logan's tongue found her clitoris. She gasped and raised her pelvis, forcing his tongue to press onto her sweet spot. She excitedly trembled under his loving touch. Her masturbatory fantasies about him paled to what she was now experiencing. The anticipation of him inside her aroused her even more.

Joyce had been a wonderful teacher when it came to instructing him on the art of cunnilingus. Logan knew exactly what he needed to do to give Jessica maximum pleasure. It was very satisfying for him to bring her to oral climax twice. However, his confidence and skill weakened when it came to sexual intercourse.

Jessica had helped to put the condom on him. She was fascinated as well as excited over his enlarged manhood standing erect like a flag-pole. She really wanted him inside her to receive as well as give plea-sure. Their first attempted joining using the missionary position was not only awkward but led to the bumping of foreheads. The second try wasn't much better. Although Jessica was wet and wanting, his attempted penetration was uncomfortable for her. He was barely halfway inside her when she had a sharp pain. She asked him to stop and withdraw. Jessica knew what the pain was from; it was the breaking of her hymen. The small trickle of blood from her vagina confirmed it. Logan didn't panic at the sight of the blood. He knew exactly what had caused it. He longingly kissed her, and then suggested that it might be easier for her to be entered if she was on top of him where she could control the depth and movement of the pene-tration.

Logan sat up and put his back against the bed's head rest. Jessica straddled him, placing herself above him while Logan held his erection in position for her. She took his manhood and placed it to her opening and gently slid him partly inside her. She cautiously moved up and down on him, slowly taking more of his engorged cock deeper into her with each downward slide. Finally, her pussy loosened and she took his whole erectness into her. Yet, their lovemaking was still cumbersome and faltered a few times. Neither knew how the other should properly move. With Joyce, Logan had just laid on his back with her hands clenched in his while she skillfully rode his cock until she reached climax, and then made sure he orgasmed. This moment for he and Jessica wasn't just sex; it was their first time together. It should be different, better, and the most memorable moment in their relationship. He felt that there should be participation between the two of them but wasn't sure how it should be done. They both self-consciously moved together but not in sync with one another's bodies. Logan accidentally pulled out of her twice, which was embarrassing to both of them. After a couple of tries they found their rhythm. As their motion became more heated, Logan became more aroused. Clutching her tight, face to face, Jessica's discovery of how to move to maximize both their pleasure was too much for him to hold back his ejaculation.

Logan moaned, "Oh, God, baby, I'm going to come."

Hearing his words was a bit disappointing. It hadn't even been ten minutes and he was about to let loose, and she was just enjoying the mounting pleasure of him inside her, though she had expected as much. She knew from health education class at school that young men were prone to orgasm quicker than a female.

He squeezed her tight, putting his head in the nape of her neck. As he released himself, he grabbed onto her buttocks and pulled her hips in as he pushed his pelvis up, pressing himself as deep as he could into her. Jessica could feel his hard cock pulse with each spurt that vigorously pumped out of him. He gasped in time with his expulsions. She wished she could have felt his release inside her. It would surely be a more pleasurable experience for the both of them, but she absolutely wouldn't risk that chance of getting pregnant. Just the thought of pushing a child out of her small vagina made her shudder, like the gruesome alien hatchling that burst out of the man's stomach in the classic sci-fi movie.

When his orgasm finally ended, he once again put his arms around her torso, then kissed the nape of her neck.

"That was," he gasped, "the most... The most..." He gently grabbed onto the back of her head and pulled her close. "The most wonderful thing I have *ever* experienced." He kissed her deeply and then gave her a loving hug. She reciprocated.

After a few minutes of embracing, Jessica noticed that Logan hadn't become flaccid as he remained inside her. She was under the impression from what she had learned the males reverted to their normal size almost immediately after ejaculation. It puzzled her. She commented with a smile, "You're still hard. Shall we do it again?"

"Am I?" he said, and then took notice. "I guess I am a bit. And yes, again and again. But I need to change the condom. I think I overfilled it."

Immediately after removing the condom, Logan's penis began to deflate. The tightness of the condom had kept his blood engorged cock upright, but now that circulation had returned, he quickly went limp. Jessica just hoped he would quickly recuperate. She wanted him inside her again and this time she hoped he wouldn't shoot his load so fast.

It only took a few minutes for Logan to react to their caressing, kissing and fondling of one another. Jessica kept stroking his erection making sure he was thoroughly aroused for another lovemaking session. This time she wanted him atop of her and in control. Logan tucked a pillow under her to raise her hips. This time he slid easily and gently into her wet opening. This time he lasted over 20 minutes. The third time it was even longer. It was nearly 1:30 a.m. and neither was tired of pleasuring one another. They wanted to have penetrative sex one more time before trying to get some sleep, but Jessica was too sore inside to receive his manhood again. Instead, they found other ways to pleasure one another. Finally, fully exhausted from their exploration and satisfying of each other, they fell asleep together. Logan held her securely with an arm under her and a hand to one breast.

The two of them had only been asleep for less than three hours when a rousing knock came to the bedroom door. It was Marc. He had come to fetch Logan as ordered if Marc could accomplish the task he was assigned.

"Come," Logan called out.

Entering, Marc saluted and said, "Apologies for the intrusion commander, but you're needed in the Puma. I've received a response. They wish to speak with you."

"I'll be there straight away," Logan confirmed and returned Marc's salute. "Dismissed."

Groggily, Jessica questioned, "You have to go already? It's not even six yet."

Logan reached out and kissed her. "I'm sorry but duty calls. Keep the bed warm for us. I'll be back shortly." He kissed her again before putting his uniform and boots on, and then called for Blaze to follow him out the door.

When Logan's business was completed, he wasn't certain it was going to have any impact on the forthcoming battle. So, he found no reason to discuss the matter with Jessica. As for Marc, he had been up all night and needed some sleep. He told Marc it wasn't necessary for him to go on the away mission. Marc told Logan he needed him on mission. Someone with experience needed to drive the Puma or the HGC, and there was only one other experienced soldier on the team, besides Logan. Logan agreed, but told him once they returned, he was to get six hours of rack time, no excuses. He needed Marc sharp for the battle.

Logan was true to his word; he returned to Jessica after briefly being away. There wasn't much time for sleep again. So, Logan beckoned her to join him in the shower, telling her it was one more thing they should share together with an uncertain future. Jessica didn't need any convincing, she knew their time together was fleeting and every moment was precious. The intimacy of their showering together turned quickly to one last act of lovemaking.

PART VII

FLAGS OF FREEDOM

LOGAN AND HIS TEAM HAD DONE EVERYTHING THEY COULD WITH THE resources available to help Jessica and her people defend their enclave. Now all that remained was to await the enemy's arrival and hope that their efforts were enough to stop the incursion.

Kristen and Luci had also done everything they could do to prep for the battle. Luci had taken up position inside an EMT vehicle that was parked along a side street, halfway between both defensive lines. She, her assistant, and her driver were the first responders that would triage any wounded, and then transport them to the hospital. Once there, Dr. Kristen Leger and her two assistants would take over. They both hoped that Logan's and Jessica's plan would be enough that there would be no serious injuries or casualties.

Benny and Logan were on the far side of the bridge in their Puma, hidden away where they had previously been positioned. Jessica took charge of the bridge defenses. She had Logan's Peacemaker and one of the extra Sig Sauer MCX Spear carbine rifles they had brought from Nevada. Barb Schwartz was perched in the highest, and closest, of the armory's watchtowers to the bridge. Logan had given her Big Mama, his sniper rifle. Barb was placed there not only to be a sniper but also to act as overwatch to supply intel on then enemy's bridge advance. Barb's assignment was a critical one. She was the person who would tell Jessica when to detonate the IEDs, so the enemy would suffer the most devastation.

Donna and Katie were in charge of stopping the enemy from getting through the fairgrounds and to More Avenue, if possible. Or at least do as much damage to the force as possible. The two of them had been issued Sig Sauer MCX Spear carbine rifles. Their job was to make sure the enemy followed the river crossing that was booby trapped with the six-pointed, sharpened steel jacks that Milan and his team had fashioned and submerged under the waterway and planted along the river's edge. The spikes would hopefully pierce the tires of some of the vehicles as they forded the river. If this worked and the enemy had to abandon their vehicles, then the ground troops hidden in the tree line would open fire. The second line of defense was a series of IEDs camouflaged in the tree break into the fairgrounds. The IEDs consisted of some drums of diesel fuel, some propane canisters, and wireless, remote controlled Claymore mines to set off the explosions. The blasts would also cause the trees to splinter and fall, hopefully on top of the enemy, in an effort to halt their advance. If the Canadians broke through that defensive line, then it was up to Katie and Donna to use the two rocket launchers Logan had given them. The last line of defense was Marc and Milan in the HGC.

On the bridge, the eight abandoned vehicles from the last Canadian assault had been repurposed. Originally, they had been maneuvered into position so they formed a winding pathway meant to make the bridge crossing a slow one. However, Logan had augmented the serpentine path. Like the IEDs used in the river defenses, Logan was using the same method with the bridge. The vehicles from mid-point to the south end had their trunks packed with propane, diesel and kerosene, and would also be ignited with Claymores at the right moment to achieve maximum destruction.

If one thing was certain, the Canadians were punctual. Five minutes before first light two columns of armored vehicles arrived. Tactical fighting vehicles were what Logan had feared. Worse, it wasn't Canadian vehicles, as Barb relayed to him. From her description the vehicles sounded like Commando II Tactical Armored Patrol Vehicles (TAPVs), which were mainly used by the UT Border Defense Force for patrolling the Canadian border wall. Although the border forces stationed around Lake Ontario and the St. Lawrence River were originally under UTA authority, the lands were now in Republic territory. Both Sovereign Trumbull and Chief Scott knew that to ask them to choose a side would be detrimental to the safety of the entire nation. The UT Border Defense Force needed to remain neutral, remain in place, and guard America from an invasion by the "Drug dealers, criminals, rapists, and other degenerates who stole our great territory of Alaska," Trumbull told the nation upon the agreement with Scott.

The Canadians were being stealthy, attacking Walton with American 4-wheeled fighting machines so no one would be the wiser if detected along the way. The good news was most TAPVs were not heavily armed. Most were turret equipped with a 40mm automatic grenade launcher and a .50 caliber machine gun in a turret (40/50s). No match for their Puma or HGC. Unfortunately, the upside also had a downside. TAPVs were constructed to provide maximum protection against mine and improvised explosive device (IED) blasts. This included the tires. This was bad news, since a great part of their defensive strategy relied on IEDs. Logan hoped the rigged devices had enough explosive power to do damage.

The two convoys did not immediately advance onto their respective battlegrounds. Logan knew they would attack as soon as it was twilight. Barb radioed to Logan that she could barely make out a few soldiers perched in the lead vehicle surveying the bridge with special focus on the bus blockade. She said that it was a long shot but at first light she could probably take one of them out if Jessica or Logan agreed. Logan told Jessica they should hold off. No use taking pot shots at the enemy and getting unwanted attention unless Barb could guarantee a kill shot, and only if she could confirm she was sniping an officer.

Lieutenant Chantal Bourhis and Captain Stephanie Armitage were standing in the wide command hatch of their command-and-control vehicle, focused on who was secured to the bus, using there night vision binoculars.

"What do you make of it, Lieutenant?" Armitage asked her subordinate.

"Looks like whoever it is must of really pissed someone off to get boot fucked like that, ma'am," she conjectured.

Armitage agreed, "Probably our spy, eh? So, the enemy knows we are coming. Get me a sitrep from Bravo, Lieutenant. I want to be back at base by 1200 hours."

"Roger that." Bourhis called into the radio, "Alpha Two to Bravo Actual. I need a sitrep," she requested.

"Alpha Two," came a male voice over the radio. "This is Bravo

Actual. We are FEBA, cocked and loaded. No sign of enemy. Awaiting orders, ma'am. Do you copy, Alpha Two?"

"Roger that, Bravo Actual. Break," Bourhis replied, telling them to wait for a moment for a response. She turned to her commander. "Bravo Actual reports they are FEBA and awaiting orders, Captain," relaying Bravo Team was on the forward edge of the battlefield.

Captain Armitage looked up to the sky. Twilight had come and with it a new month and impending rain storm. "Let's git'r done, Lieutenant. Permission to engage enemy with extreme prejudice. And get those busses out of our way."

"Affirmative, Captain," Bourhis acknowledged, and then relayed the orders to both attack units.

From behind Captain Armitage's vehicle came two Commando II Select 90mm Direct Fire Vehicles (DFVs). Pulling forward the two 90mm low-pressure cannon armored vehicles began to hammer the school busses. The two tactical DFVs blew the busses apart with ease, separating them from one another, and opening up a gap for the column to pass through. What remained of Madanello was only bits and pieces.

The sound of cannon fire was unmistakable to Logan, the explosions of which reverberated across the river and to Barstow's Feed & Seed. He didn't need to see what their target had been, he was certain it was the main bridge obstacle—the busses. He also knew that what was firing at the busses weren't regular TAPVs. Logan called to Jessica and Barbara and warned them not to let any cannon vehicle cross the bridge. If they did it would be disastrous. He said the Puma would be on the way and would take out any cannon vehicles that were in the rear of the column, as soon as the bridge IEDs were triggered.

Leading the advancing bridge column was one of the two 90mm DFVs, followed by six TAPV 40/50s, and finally Captain Armitage and Lieutenant Bourhis in the Command & Control vehicle. Only the second 90mm DFV stayed behind to guard the rear flank.

The lead DFV moved cautiously across the bridge nudging the strategically placed vehicle obstructions out of the way, so their advancing column could have a direct route to the other side. From what Barb was describing from her perch, Jessica was certain the Canadians were going to prematurely set off their booby traps.

The DFV was significantly ahead of the other vehicles and would reach the busses before the others. As the middle six vehicles were finally in the right position, Jessica triggered the IEDs. The bridge erupted with six simultaneous balls of fire. The blasts were so fierce that three smaller cars flipped into the air. The backend of one car came crashing down onto a TAPV, while another came down hitting the front side of another, forcing the TAPV through the concrete bridge railing into the river below. The third car flipped over the low concrete guardrail and off the bridge. Most of the TAPVs were unaffected by the eruptions, and they pushed forward through the raging fires.

The 90mm DFV had just reached the breach in the busses when Jessica had unleashed the firestorm on the bridge, but the cannon vehicle was too far ahead of the column to be affected. Barb pulled the trigger of the AT6 86mm rocket launcher, just as it came through the bus barricade and bore down on the vehicles blockading the armory. The cab of the cannon vehicle tore apart under the explosion, but continued its forward motion until it rammed into the car barricade and stopped. None of Jessica's people had been injured in the crash. However the AT6 rocket hadn't killed all the occupants. Out of the backend of the burning vehicle came three angry Canadians, who immediately opened fire with deadly consequences. After killing three of Jessica's people, Jessica's line broke. A few of the barricade support fighters began to flee, only to find themselves shot in the back. Barb took one of the Canadians out but the other two she couldn't get in the cross hairs of her scope. Both soldiers were on the far side of the truck, and the smoke and flames were also obscuring her line of sight. As the two soldiers made it to the car barricade, the 90mm DFV erupted in a loud explosion. The vehicle ripped apart from the ordinance and fuel that finally ignited, sending fragments of metal and a percussion wave in a 360 degree path of destruction. The two soldiers were struck down, along with two of Jessica's fighters suffering injuries.

***

Ninety seconds after Logan heard the bridge IEDs explode, the Puma drove out the alleyway that paralleled the river onto the intersection of Water and Bridge Streets. The Commando II 90mm Direct Fire Vehicle was no more than 50 feet from their position when the Puma emerged. The Canadians weren't stupid when it came to their rear defense; they were ready for any flanking countermeasures. If Benny had pulled completely into the center of Bridge Street and stopped, the enemy's cannon would have been aligned dead center with the Puma. Seeing the awaiting vehicle as they appeared, Benny didn't stop short of center but instead stopped long of center.

Logan had already been standing in the open turret hatch when the Puma cut across the street and stopped. Logan turned to fire his AT6, just as the enemy's weapon's station began to move toward them. The Canadians didn't wait to fire. Their first shot hit the back of the mission module. The Puma shuddered as the rear end was forced back a few feet. Logan nearly dropped the rocket launcher but held steady, and then pulled the trigger just as the cannon vehicle took another shot. Both vehicle's rounds struck each other's within a split second of one another. Logan's vehicle took another hard hit, this time to the center of the mission module, setting it ablaze. Logan's rocket did the same, but his round struck the enemy's gun turret. The munitions inside ignited and blew the vehicle apart.

Logan had not been quick enough to get under cover. A piece of flying shrapnel pierced through the body armor of his upper left chest and punctured him deeply. He fell down into the turret and almost off the turret perch.

Hearing the commotion, Benny turned to see. Spotting the jagged piece of metal protruding from his chest, he exclaimed, "Shit, Logan. You're hit!"

Before Logan could respond, something exploded on the outside of the vehicle. It was followed by another explosion. Neither blast pene-trated the Puma's hull. Logan struggled to rise up as Benny backed up the vehicle and turned to face whatever was shooting at them. From the shielded heavy machine gun station, Logan saw a TAPV charging toward them. It was the Canadian Command and Control vehicle firing its 40mm grenade launcher. He called through his radio headset, "TAPV coming at us." Logan unleashed the vehicle's Patriot six-barrel rotary machine gun as the Puma sped toward the oncoming enemy vehicle.

Another 40mm grenade hit the Puma. This time it was to the gun station. The explosion took out the Patriot and shattered the bullet resistant windshield of the turret. Logan was peppered with glass frag-ments. If it hadn't been for him wearing protective shooting glasses, the tiny shards would have torn into his eyes, blinding him. This time he fell off the turret perch and landed near Benny. In a bloody mess Logan ordered, "Ram the son-of-shit-biscuit off the bridge."

Benny put his foot down on the accelerator and sped toward the enemy.

As the first Commando II 90mm Direct Fire Vehicle rolled across the bridge pushing the cars out of the way, the flanking attack had already begun. That first DFV had reached the opposite river bank. The spikes in the water had not stopped it, but it had slowed it to a crawl since its tires were shredded.

From the tree line Donna aimed her AT6 rocket launcher at the cannon vehicle. The rocket hit the vehicle's engine compartment, destroying it and killing everyone inside. The force of the rocket leaving its tube knocked Donna from her shooter's kneeling position. Katie was hurriedly trying to get her to her feet, when the trees around them began to splinter under the fire of the enemy's .50 caliber machine guns. They both dashed away unscathed, so they thought, to their next position. Katie didn't notice the large splinter in her thigh until the adrenalin began to wear off. She yanked it from her leg and gave it a quick field dressing. The enemy was still advancing.

Out of the eight river crossing vehicles, two had now been disabled, one from the AT6, and another from the spikes. This did not stop the Canadians in their advance. The remainder of the column re-routed, following their side of the river bank to a secondary crossing almost directly across from the tree break. Milan's team had not planted any spikes in that part of the river. Circumventing the remainder of the spikes, the Canadians cut across the river and to the tree break that led to the fairgrounds.

The break in the trees wasn't substantial but plenty wide for the TAPVs to pass through. As the new lead vehicle broke through, Danny detonated their second line of defense. A large fireball erupted all around the first and second enemy vehicles. The trees on both sides of the break tore apart at their bases and toppled, as a large fire fed by diesel fuel engulfed the second vehicle. The trees were not the only booby trap that had been placed. Just after the tree break, several drums of diesel fuel and propane canisters had been buried with six inches of dirt atop them. The lead vehicle upended as it passed over the massive eruption, tearing its undercarriage apart, disabling it. From a secondary group of trees, Katie, Donna, Danny, and the team members opened fire on the lead vehicle as a few soldiers tried to escape the burning wreckage.

There was a rapid succession of explosions. They were aimed near the TAPV that was trapped under the fallen trees. The trees disinte-grated under the cannon fire. Another 90mm DFV appeared leading the remainder of the armored vehicle column, Driving over the pulverized tree remains and through the blaze, they unleashed a maelstrom of weapons fire. The defensive line was broken. Panicked, most of the team ran in different directions. The vehicles sped onto the fairground, spraying .50 caliber weapons fire in all directions. Katie's and Donna's teams were being cut down.

Katie and Donna made it to an out building, but Danny had not followed. Machine gun fire ripped through the building as the two ducked for cover. Katie still had an AT6 with her, but she and Donna were pinned down. She radioed the HGC.

Marc and Milan understood they were now the last line of defense. As the TAPV column converged onto their position, Milan quickly moved the vehicle from its hiding place and into the direct path of the oncoming enemy.

There was no way for the enemy to go around the HGC. There were large maple trees to the HGC's left and right. If the enemy tried to use Fair Street, which was just slightly south, they would find the tractor trailer blocking the roadway, augmented by other vehicles filling the gaps between trees and yards, that would stall their advance.

Marc had his AT6 out but just as he aimed it, the enemy's cannon let loose with a barrage of shots. The HGC's cabin and gun station tore apart under the heavy fire of 90mm gun. Marc's rocket shot into the air as the HGC exploded into flames. Milan and Marc had no chance for escape.

The lead enemy vehicle swung right, like it was headed toward Fair Street, but it wasn't. The entire column turned around and, in a hurry, headed back the way they came. At first, Katie thought they were coming back for Donna and her. They were about to dart to another building when they realized the enemy was heading back to the river. Katie still had her AT6, and wanted to blow the cannon vehicle to hell for killing Milan and Marc, but the 90mm DFV had already moved out of target range.

From around the corner of the building the two of them had taken refuge in, Katie watched as the last vehicle in the column turned its gun station forward from its rear watch position. She aimed the rocket launcher, exhaled, and then said, "Up yours, motherfuckers!"

Katie didn't miss.

Captain Armitage had received an urgent call from Fort Drum command that the Americans were attacking the base, and almost every military installation they had seized control of. Command told

Armitage to immediately withdraw from Walton and return to base to help defend it. Armitage was just about to seize control of Walton, but she wouldn't disregard the orders of a superior. The lives of Canadians were worth more than wiping out a bunch of American civilians and a few leftover civil war soldiers. She recalled her troops and told them to rendezvous at Delaware and Townsend Streets.

She had anticipated a quick withdrawal from the battle zone, but couldn't fathom how a Puma fighting vehicle that wasn't even heavily armed could have gotten the upper hand over a cannon vehicle. Now it was up to her and her Command & Control team to get the job done, and the enemy Puma was bearing down on them.

Barb saw the Puma ram the TAPV head on, just as the rain started to pour down. There was an immense loud crash. The backend of the TAPV reared up. Then slammed down onto the bridge, shaking it. Barb called to Jessica and told her what had just happened. One of the other fleeing TAPVs pulled up to the wrecked Command & Control vehicle. Soldiers from the stopped TAPV moved to the wreckage, and opened the back door. Barb looked through her scope, and as soon as the first survivor was being pulled out, Barb pulled the trigger.

The back of Capt Stephanie Armitage's head tore apart, spraying blood and brain matter back into the wrecked vehicle. The two enemy soldiers were shocked. They ducked for cover, searching cautiously for the shooter. Lt Chantal Bourhis stumbled out of the crew compartment, dazed and unaware of the sniper that had just taken out her commander. As a soldier attempted to pull her from the doorway, another shot came. There was no noise of a bullet being fired, only the thud of the impact when it hit Bourhis in the throat. The two grabbed Bourhis and pulled her toward the rescue vehicle. With one parting shot, Barb struck one of them in the back. The TAPV took off, never attempting return fire.

Jessica was screaming into her radio for her mother as she knelt over Logan. Battered and hurt himself, Benny had dragged Logan from the burning Puma and a safe distance away before it exploded.

Laying on the wet pavement under the drenching rain, Logan looked up to Jessica with glassy eyes and tried to say something. She leaned in. Hearing his words, she reached into a pocket of his tactical vest and retrieved a small box. Opening it, Jessica found a diamond engagement ring.

Jessica teared up and lovingly told him, "You're such an asshat," and then warned him in a scolding tone, "Logan Ross, don't you dare die on me. Don't you dare."

Logan mustered all his remaining strength and choked out, "Thank you."

Jessica, Kristen, Luci, along with Blaze had been gathered on the open front porch of the Ross family home discussing family matters, when Blaze sat up and growled warningly. A moment after, three tactical military vehicles came down the drive. All three women were armed with assault rifles and pistols, and ready to meet any threat if necessary.

When the combat vehicles pulled close to the house, a soldier in the gunner's station stood up within the open hatch waving a white flag.

"Please pardon the intrusion, ladies. We were told by Katie Troy in Walton that we could find First Sergeant Logan Ross and his team here. My commanding officer would like to speak with them. Permission to disembark, ma'am," he addressed Jessica, who was in the front of her group with her hand on Logan's Peacemaker that was strapped to her hip.

Jessica replied, "You may, unarmed, or not at all."

The soldier spoke into his radio headset, and within a moment, two officers came out of the armored carrier, unarmed as requested.

The higher-ranking officer addressed Jessica, "My name is Lieutenant Colonel Matthew Spoth." Gesturing, he then introduced his subordinate Captain Eden Tootil. "We were told by Katie Troy in

Walton, NY that we would find Jessica Miranda at this residence, who could put us in contact with First Sergeant Ross and his team. Are you Ms. Miranda, First Sergeant Ross's fiancée?"

"I am. And what can I do for you?"

"Is First Sergeant Ross home? We would like to extend our gratitude for the radio call we received three weeks ago. If it wasn't for him and his team, we wouldn't have known about the Canadian incursion until it was too late. Thanks to his team we were able to rout them and regain our key military installations along the border wall and the Erie Canal."

"*Really?*" Jessica asked with astonishment. "He didn't tell me he made contact with Republic forces."

"Yes, ma'am. Now would First Sergeant Ross be home?"

"Yes," Jessica confirmed, and then added. "He's always home. If you follow me, please."

Jessica escorted them to the back of the house and showed them the grave markers. Besides the ones for Logan's mother and father, there were three other markers with names on them. All three had the same memorial inscription, "Died with honor. Battle of Walton NY. May 1, 2054. Seeing the names, Sgt Marc Romano, CW2 Milan Crncevic, and 1Sg Logan Ross, Lt Col Spoth turned to his subordinate and ordered, "Flags, Captain. We need three flags for these fallen heroes." As Captain Tootil departed, Spoth commented, "I'm very sorry for your loss, Ms. Miranda. Is there any of the first sergeant's team alive?"

Jessica returned, "Does it matter? The war is long over. Let the dead rest and those who survived move on."

The colonel answered her. "I was sent on behalf of President Scott, former Chief of The Republic. I have been authorized to offer the first sergeant and his team warrant officer promotions along with a proposal to serve The United Republic of America in a new capacity. That's what our country is now called. The president intends to rebuild our nation but it will take time. Canada sees us as weak and vulnerable. President Scott wanted the first sergeant and his team to take charge of our Northeast border force. The President feels that after the exceptional job they did at securing the Hoover Dam, and of course their exemplary duty in the Battle of Dubuque, that they were the only choice for the task."

Captain Tootil returned with three flags and held them out. Taking them, the colonel continued, "Ms. Miranda, please accept these three flags of our new nation, as a symbol of our respect and gratitude for these three outstanding soldiers and what they did for their country. Their sacrifices will not be forgotten." Jessica accepted the colonel's symbolic gesture. Then the colonel turned to the grave markers and ordered, "Attention!" He raised his hand in salute, Tootil following his lead, and then announced, "Thank you for your service." Tootil repeated her commander's words. "At ease," Spoth declared. Then they both gave a salute.

Lieutenant Colonel Spoth turned to Jessica and said, "Ma'am, if there is anything I or The United Republic of America can do for you, I'll be at Fort Drum for the next 60 days. Please feel free to come find me."

"Actually," Jessica said. "There is something."

Three hours after Lt Col Spoth departed with his team, another vehicle came up the driveway. This time Blaze did not growl a warning but instead barked and wagged his tail. From out of the pickup came Benny Lee and Neil Hawkins. Jessica greeted Benny with a hug and then moved to Hawkins and planted a very passionate lip kiss on him.

"You two missed some important visitors today," Jessica told them as they walked to the porch.

"We heard," Hawkins replied at the same time Kristen beckoned Benny, "Come here and kiss me like you miss me, soldier." Benny did.

Jessica asked, "How did you hear?"

"Benny and I stopped by Walton to see how Danny was doing. Katie gave us a report," he said.

"I could have told you how he was doing," Kristen told Hawkins.

"Yeah, I know," he replied, "but you telling me isn't the same as seeing him."

Hawkins slightly struggled to sit. Kristen saw his discomfort. "So, what did the soldiers want?"

"Where's the sling you're supposed to be wearing, Commander?" Kristen asked Hawkins. She then ordered, "Off with the shirt and let's check the wound."

"Don't commander me," Hawkins warned. "I've declared my independence," he added. "The name is Hawkins. Neil Hawkins."

"Another new name?" Jessica asked, exasperated.

"He came up with that one on the way back from Marc's memorial service," Benny told them.

Jessica knelt down to Hawkins, and unequivocally told him "Logan. You know we all love you, but no one is going to call you, Neil Hawkins, Phil Garcia, or Rick Helm."

"Oh, you should have heard his first new name of the day," Benny announced. "Robert 'Pigpen' Hart."

"Okay, that was a terrible amalgamation," Logan admitted. "But Neil Hawkins. That's a keeper. Neil Young, Ron Hawkins. Two great Canadian musicians."

"Wrong," Benny corrected him. "Neil Young became a dual citizen in 2020. So, he was technically Canarican."

"My two favorite Canadian *born* musicians, then."

"All good," Kristen told him after examining his healing wound. "And by the way, you do realize Jessica will never marry anyone else but Logan Ross."

"Oh, I'm not even going to marry Logan Ross," she declared. "Not until he proposes."

Logan was shocked at the revelation. "What do you mean, I didn't propose? What's the ring on your finger mean, then?"

It was true, Logan hadn't officially proposed marriage. Even though Jessica had accepted the engagement ring, she was hoping that he would give her a proper, traditional proposal of marriage.

"Gifting me a bloody ring as you're dying isn't a proposal, it's a bequeathment."

"Oh, no you didn't!?" Benny exclaimed.

Kristen shook her head and remarked, "Logan, you really are clueless."

"Cut me some slack," Logan begged. "I died."

"Yeah, and you got the grave marker to prove it," Benny sarcastically reminded him.

"Damn, what does a dead guy gotta do to get some respect around here?" Logan asked, frustrated.

Luci came through the porch door carrying a tray of ice tea. "Propose," she told Logan, and then added, "And stop pretending you're dead; there's no need, especially after today."

Logan knew he was wrong on all accounts. He got down on one knee and gave Jessica a proper marriage proposal. Jessica accepted, and everyone cheered the romantic moment. Logan had to be helped up from his kneeling. His deep wound had not fully healed and it was uncomfortable and painful at times with certain movements.

"Damn, love is hard on the knees," he commented as both Kristen and Jessica got him back in the chair. "Now what did the soldiers want?"

Jessica explained their encounter, and then stated, "You never told me you made contact."

"Because I didn't want anyone to get their hopes up. And I was right," he told them nodding knowingly. "And now they come to offer us promotions as a consolation. What about all those who died in Walton? What do they get?" Logan bitterly asked. "I don't need their charity. I'm done, I tell you. Done. Let First Sergeant Ross stay dead and buried."

"So, you don't want their charity, then?" Jessica asked, needing confirmation of Logan's declaration. "Then I should send the three ammo boxes of 338 back?"

"What?" Logan questioned, almost like he had heard Jessica incorrectly. "338? You got 338 Norma Magnum ammo? How?"

"Well, Lieutenant Colonel Spoth did ask if there was anything he could do for me. So, I asked. But if you don't want it, I'm sure I can find another community that would be in need."

Logan remembered the words he had said to her in the den not too long ago. He smiled and returned, "Well, since they don't seem to need it, I'm sure we could put it to use."

"I thought so," Jessica said with a smile, and then kissed him.

Logan's face lit with excitement. "I got it!" he shouted. "Ryan Tedder!"

Jessica put a hand to her face and shook her head with disappointment. "We're really going to have to work on that asshat issue."

ABOUT THE AUTHOR

TS Alan is an American author of horror, supernatural fiction, and suspense, but also frequently incorporates elements of fantasy, science fiction, mystery, and satire. Alan has published four novels, and eight short stories.

As influences on his writing, Alan lists Clive Barker, Dean Koontz, Stephen King, Edgar Allen Poe, and O. Henry, among others.

Alan is also the co-founder of the entertainment website Zombie Education Alliance (zombieeducationalliance.com).

His writing credits also include two short stories published in *Devolution Z* magazine, a short published in an anthology called *What Went Wrong? (Legendary Stories)*, and shorts published in anthologies called *Whispers of the Apoc* and *Silence of the Apoc*, and others.

For more information visit TS Alan at: www.tsalan.com

www.ingramcontent.com/pod-product-compliance
Lightning Source LLC
Chambersburg PA
CBHW061203170626
46809CB00003B/1228